Astral Guardians

CHASING THE STORM

ALIYAH BURKE

Chasing the Storm
ISBN # 978-1-78430-089-0
©Copyright Aliyah Burke 2014
Cover Art by Posh Gosh ©Copyright May 2014
Interior text design by Claire Siemaszkiewicz
Totally Bound Publishing

Published in 2014 by Totally Bound Publishing, Newland House, The Point, Weaver Road, Lincoln, LN6 3QN, United Kingdom.

Totally Bound Publishing is an imprint of Total-E-Ntwined Limited.

Totally Bound Publishing books by Aliyah Burke:

Through the Fire
Seducing Damian

Code of Honour
A Marriage of Convenience
The Lieutenant's Ex-Wife
A Man Like No Other
When Stars Collide

In Aeternum
Casanova in Training
Harbour of Refuge
Protected by Shadows

Interludes
Temporary Home
Alone With You

Keeper of the Stars
Keeper of the Stars: Part One
Keeper of the Stars: Part Two
Keeper of the Stars: Part Three
Keeper of the Stars: Part Four
Keeper of the Stars: Part Five

Astral Guardians
Chasing the Storm

What's her Secret?
Preconception

CHASING THE STORM

Dedication

Thanks to Totally Bound for giving me the
opportunity to have another series with them.
To my readers, thank you for the amazing and
unending support, it's completely humbling.
I hope you enjoy Cale and Taylor's story.
To my husband, who's always there for me, I love
you.
To my parents who always encouraged me to follow
my heart and believed in me even when I didn't,
thank you.
And, as always, last but never least, my heartfelt
thanks to the men and women who serve their
country. God Bless you and your families for your
unselfish sacrifices!

The parts to waken the world's hope have been scattered far and wide to the winds and throughout the stars.

It is from there the chosen ones are marked, becoming Astral Guardians.

Alone, their individual defeat has a greater chance than when paired with the amaranthine and genuine love of their mate.

Those Guardians must find, defend and bind the pieces to call forth the hope of the world.

It will take courage, strength, love and sacrifice.

If the Guardians fail, swift death will arrive to the one who calms the beasts.

With this outcome, the world shall descend into darkness, chaos and anarchy.

Chapter One

The cold winds bit into Cale's skin as he careened down the mountain, barely missing the trees as they whipped by him. He loved it, the freedom of skiing. Above him, he spied the silhouette of the chopper that had dropped him off higher than the tree line. Just how he liked it. Cale loved utilizing a chopper to carry him high up into the mountains—it assisted his adrenaline rush when he raced back down to the base. Seeing it as it flew away made him realize even more just how alone he was up here. He wouldn't have it any other way.

Some may prefer to vacation along the beaches and soak up the rays beside women wearing next to nothing. Personally, he liked the snow, and women who wanted to do something other than tan and have people deliver them drinks.

Which could very well explain why he didn't have a girlfriend. He zigged and zagged around the trees, waiting until the last moment to change direction, cutting it as close as possible.

He was tired by the time he made it back down the mountain. In a good way, but tired. Skis in hand, he slowly strolled to the lodge, smoke rolling from its stacks reminding him how warm it would be inside. He put his things away then headed back down to the main floor where he went to the bar. Drink order in, he waited and looked about the room.

There were two men in one corner who had him immediately suspicious. He was typically very easy going, but there was something about them that had him watching them with much more caution. They wore the correct things yet they still didn't fit. He knew they were full humans and not demons, or the like which carried the rank scent of sulfur. His drink arrived and he promptly put them out of his mind.

In a chair by the window, he stared out over the slopes and smiled. This was his last day of vacation and he had every intention of enjoying himself. And he held true to that. By the time he boarded his plane a day later, he was exhausted and looking forward to the long flight so he could get some rest.

Those same two men boarded and walked past him. He didn't like the warning ripples that exploded out from him. His instincts weren't wrong about people, and not ignoring them had been his reason for survival more often than not as a teen. He wasn't about to ignore his instincts now, either. Acting as if he needed something from his bag, he located where they were and memorized their looks. He again took his seat and closed his eyes, but he was as alert as he'd ever been.

"You're nervous, Cale. Everything okay?"

The sound of his foster sister in his head calmed him instantly. *"How do you manage to feel everything we do, Dracen?"*

A light chuckle echoed in his mind. *"Thankfully it's not everything, but you're seriously on edge. Where are you?"*

"Flying home. Where are you? Hot date?"

"Mind yourself, Cale. It's late here. Everyone's sleeping."

"Except you." A fact that worried him. Dracen, of all his siblings, seemed to sleep the least. Especially recently. There'd been dark circles beneath her eyes last he'd seen her and he would bet anything that hadn't changed in the time he'd been gone.

"Obviously not me if I'm talking to you. Now tell me why you're nervous."

"There were two men at the lodge who didn't fit and now they're on the plane with me. I can't explain why I feel it, I just do."

"You never have to explain it, Cale. We all understand."

"I will be just fine, Dracen. Don't worry. You need to get some sleep. Or do I have to tell on you?"

"We're no longer teens, Cale. Tattling won't have any effect."

He smirked and crossed his arms. *"It will if I tell Tiarnán."*

"Low blow."

"Yet apparently necessary."

Tiarnán was the eldest of the foster children who'd been taken in by Lian Yang who had stayed. Throughout the decades, Lian had sheltered many. Most of those had left when they reached eighteen or twenty. Of those currently there now, even ones who'd stayed past eighteen, he and Dracen had been there the longest, while Cale had been there seven years, arriving at age fourteen. Full of anger, mistrust and suspicion. It had been bumpy for a while but soon, something had clicked in his head and he'd realized this man, Lian, was different from everyone else he'd been sent to.

They were his family now.

"Be careful, Cale."

"Always am, sister."

The connection broke. It was odd to him, being able to talk with his siblings this way. He couldn't do it other than with the other five who were different, like him. They were a unique bunch, whom Lian said had bigger challenges ahead. For the moment, there were only six of them who'd stayed after becoming of legal age. There were plenty of younger children, who they all chipped in helping with, but none older than eighteen except him and his five that he could communicate telepathically with whenever he wished.

He smiled at the airline attendant when she served him his food. Thankfully there was no one seated in his row, so he took the seat by the window and angled himself to where he could see behind him more. He wasn't about to be caught off guard.

Cale ate slowly, watching the attendants move back and forth making sure everyone was looked after. One woman stopped before him and he didn't realize he was staring until she cleared her throat.

"I'm sorry," he said with a blush.

"Can I get you something else to drink?"

Lord, she was pretty thing. "Coke please. With ice."

She flashed a grin. "Right away."

He could see himself spending some nights with her. With another flirtatious smile, he took his drink then watched her walk away. *Nice legs.* Another woman, a passenger this time, walked by and he couldn't even begin to explain the punch to his gut that happened. As if all air had been sucked from his lungs, he bent over with a wheeze.

She barely paused, just flicked a glance at him. Then she frowned and stepped closer. "Are you okay?" Her voice was low and melodic.

"Choked on my drink," he managed to say once he'd gotten some air back in his lungs. "Went down wrong."

Her smile lit up her face and he found himself returning it. "I'm sorry. Glad you're feeling better." She leaned forward a bit and her necklace fell free from her shirt.

He was riveted on the pendant. Gold, elegant in a way he'd never seen before. The symbol on it was one he'd seen before but couldn't quite place. Everything within him wanted to yank it off her and keep it for himself. Keep it next to him, against his own flesh. His back burned and he shifted in his seat.

"Have a great flight." She moved by him and he craned his neck behind to see where she went.

The woman had to pass the two men who made him uncomfortable. And the way they watched her and shared a look only increased his feeling. Possessiveness flowed through him — problem was, he didn't know if it was toward the woman or the pendant.

He leaned back and barely moved when the attendant came by to take his trash. His heart rate wouldn't slow and all he could see was that small gold disc, which hung on a filigree chain around her neck.

Edgy the entire flight back, he got more antsy when they landed. Taking his bag, he was in the front of the pack to disembark. However, he waited against the walkway wall for the woman to appear. She did so, pulling a purple, leopard-print suitcase behind her. It was more like a backpack with a handle and wheels.

Her clothing conservative, hair as well. There was nothing about her that screamed 'look at me', yet he couldn't take his eyes off her.

Behind her, the two men appeared and his gaze narrowed. Stepping before her, he watched her sidestep to avoid hitting him and carry on without looking up. It was then he realized she had earbuds in and was listening to something. So he fell into step beside her, cautious of where the two men were behind them.

Her strides were purposeful and he liked that she didn't take small dainty steps, as if her legs were in cuffs. That sent an image through his head, which he wasn't so quick to vanquish.

The moment they stepped out into the hall of the airport, she looked sideways at him. Her eyes grew wide and she slowed as she took one bud out of her ear.

"Weren't you ahead of me?"

He flashed his flirty grin. "Guess you caught up to me." He stared at her neck, wanting to see the pendant again.

"Really? Guess so." Her disbelief was palpable.

Cale shrugged easily. The men behind them had stopped as well, talking amongst themselves yet obviously waiting for them to continue. Honestly, he hadn't a clue which one of them they were after now. He couldn't let her face them alone, though.

"Care to share a taxi?"

"You don't even know where I'm going."

"You're right. How about a coffee, we talk then share a taxi."

Her laughter made him smile even more.

Taylor Kenyon wasn't quite sure what to make of the man standing before her. He amused her. And given how he didn't make her skin crawl, like those two following her did, maybe he would convince them she wasn't an easy target.

"Coffee sounds wonderful."

He raked a hand through his dark brown hair and gave her a nod. "Excellent."

They fell into step and made their way through to the concessions. She watched him out of the corner of her eye.

An athlete. He was fit and had a nice movement to him. Looked good, too. Tanned skin, dark hair, killer smile. She almost shook her head but managed to stop herself at the last minute. A man wasn't anything she needed in her life right now.

"Preference on where to go?"

We can definitely add nice voice to his list as well. "I don't have one."

They settled on a place and she got some hot tea while he got a cappuccino. She picked a seat by the window where she could have her back at a corner and look out past the man with her to those milling about. It didn't help her nerves when she saw the same two creeps hanging out.

Stirring the sugar into her tea, she stared at the man sharing the table with her. He had incredible blue eyes which were focused intently on her. She blinked. "Something on my face?"

"Just wondering about your necklace."

Warning spiked up her spine. But she didn't lose her composure, it wasn't in her to do so. "What about it?" She sipped the brew and wished she were able to truly enjoy it.

"It's unique. Where did you get it?"

"My grandmother gave it to me before she died." She touched the chain but didn't reveal the pendant. "She told me it would bring me luck." A sorrowful laugh. "I'm still waiting on that. But it's part of her and I love it for that reason alone."

Her grandmother had said a whole lot of other things, but she wasn't going to share them with this man. He didn't ask to see it, which had her wondering if perhaps he *wasn't* another after her. A thought that was nice, although brief, for it vanished when he looked in the direction of the two men who'd definitely been after her.

I have to get away from him.

"What's your name?" he asked. "Just realized we haven't been introduced to one another."

"Taylor."

"Cale. Cale Mattox."

Another practiced smile. "Nice to meet you." She drank more of her tea and chatted with him about being in France. He'd been skiing, as she'd been. Same lodge, and how surprising it was they hadn't run into each other there. "Excuse me, I need to use the facilities."

"Then we can get a taxi."

She stood and gripped the handle of her suitcase. "I still have to go to baggage claim. We could meet there."

He sent another glance to where she knew the men were. "Sounds good to me. See you in a bit, Taylor."

Not if I have anything to say about it. She gave a nod and walked to the nearest bathroom. She sank against the wall and rubbed her arms as she tried to figure out what step to take next.

"You okay, sweetie?" A cleaning lady asked her.

"No. There are two men following me and they're making me really nervous. I also think another man is, but I'm not positive."

The woman's face grew dark and thunderous. She pulled a radio off her belt and spoke into it. "What do they look like?"

She gave the men's description and after a brief hesitation, gave Cale's as well. If it was only her imagination that had her thinking he was with them, well, that was her mistake. But she couldn't risk it.

A female officer showed up in the bathroom and they left together. She saw two more uniforms talking to the men. All three. One on the two and one on Cale. She didn't make eye contact just allowed the woman to escort her.

"Do you need to get any luggage?"

"No, ma'am. This is all I have. Just need to grab a taxi."

"I'll stay with you until you do."

"Thank you."

"Just doing our job." True to her word, the lady didn't leave her side until she closed the door of the cab.

"The Hilton, please." She leaned back as the driver pulled out and merged into the busy airport traffic. Lord, her nerves were shot. She closed her eyes and willed the stress to drain from her. Didn't quite work, but when he parked before the hotel, she felt marginally better.

After paying him, she thanked him as she climbed out. Gripping her handle, she walked into the lobby and up to the front desk to get a room. Hopefully—it wasn't anything she'd set up ahead of time. Thankfully they had space and she was soon soaking in the tub with a glass of wine beside her.

The men were not the usual ones she'd seen since her grandmother had passed. They were Caucasian and Hispanic instead of black—perhaps her cousins had hired other men. All she knew was she was exhausted, and needed a few days of not racing across the globe.

Suddenly nervous, she rose and wrapped up in her robe before taking her glass of wine with her to stand in front of the large window that offered her a lovely view of Seattle. This was a nice city—maybe she could lose herself in it. At least for a little while.

She called down to the front desk for a paper and some food. While she waited for those to be delivered, she changed into one of her few outfits and briskly ran a towel over her head, drying her new short haircut. She'd just done it and the dye job in the hotel.

Staring at her reflection, she touched the shorn locks and sighed heavily. Her hair had been long and one of her vanity points. So she'd chopped it off in order to help her escape detection. She patted the style. Textured short layers with a long neckline, short sideburns and a slightly diagonal fringe. It had red streaks through it, which kind of reminded her of flames. Different, that was for sure.

"It'll grow on me," she told herself. "I just have to figure out why they want this thing so bad."

Taylor lifted the pendant and stared at it. Delicate. Intricate. And gold, but for the life of her she couldn't pinpoint why they wanted it so bad. "They can't truly think this will bring them treasure beyond their wildest dreams." Meeting her own gaze she shook her head. "Remember who we're talking about. They may believe that."

Whatever it was, it was enough for them to try to kill her for it. And that had eradicated any thought she'd once had of giving it to them. To be honest, she wasn't sure they wouldn't still kill her after they had it.

Her musings were broken by a knock on the door. "Room service."

She opened the door and paid for the food. Ignoring the table, she spread out on the bed, food to her left as she opened the paper to the classifieds. As she finished off the last of her dessert, she had several options circled for both apartments and jobs. Given the time of day, she would call in the morning. Placing the tray outside the door, she looked up and down the quiet hall. Then back in her room, she locked the door and engaged the chain.

Curtains drawn and lights off, she went to bed. The sleep helped her immensely and when she woke at six, she felt so much better. She had the place for one more night, yet she still took her bag with her as she headed down to get a spot of breakfast. After she'd finished and had paid her bill, she had the bellhop secure her a cab to take care of her business for the day.

The taxi took her through the neighborhoods of the circled apartments—she wanted a look at the surrounding areas before she even tried for one. When she'd paid the driver and stepped out before the first job location, she had one apartment picked out. Sure, she'd not even seen the inside, but she needed a place to stay where she felt safe. If the actual rental was subpar she wouldn't take it, but the other places she wouldn't stay based on location. Avoiding her cousins because they wanted to kill her was defeated if she was killed trying to get back to her place.

Spying a pay phone, she went to it to call the landlord and set up a meeting to view the apartment. Then she called the job and set up a time to come for an interview. After all that, she walked to one of the numerous coffee shops on the street corners and sat outside while she waited for time to pass.

* * * *

Taylor got the apartment and took the job at the small diner. That night, she ate dinner in her new place. It wasn't furnished and she ate out of the takeout containers, but she'd had a bed delivered and had gotten some new sheets for the bed. Other things would come in time. In the meantime, she would tuck her head in and blend in best she could. That worked wonders until the night she came home from a double shift and found someone on the steps waiting for her.

Cale Mattox stood when she approached. His blue eyes pierced her and he arched an eyebrow. "Good thing I'm a forgiving type of man. Care to tell me why the TSA guy detained me?"

"How did you find me?" *If he did, would the others?*

"I asked first." Some of her panic must have shown on her face for he immediately held up his hands. "I'm not going to hurt you, Taylor. I promise."

Funny how she believed him. It didn't make sense, but she got a warm, safe feeling from him. Not one that had her looking for the nearest exit. "Can we talk inside?"

His smile was sin. Pure, raw, sexual sin. "Anything you want."

Chapter Two

Cale watched the woman who'd allowed him into her apartment, no matter how reluctantly. He'd known she was suspicious of him but to actually have him detained, okay, he'd not thought she had it in her.

"Can I get you something to drink?"

"Whatever you're having," he said. Pivoting around in a circle, he took in the apartment. Not much to speak of. Bare necessities but clean.

A bottle of Coke appeared before him and after he took it from her, she waved him into the small living room where she sat in an overstuffed chair that had definitely seen better days. He took the couch where he could see her and the door.

"Care to tell me what that was all about?" He opened his drink and took a nice long swig.

"Did Jeremy send you?"

He blinked a few times. "Who's Jeremy?"

Her sigh was telling. "I'm sorry about earlier. My cousin has sent men after me. He wants the pendant from my grandmother. He and the others are under the foolish belief it will bring them all the treasure they could ever want."

"Why didn't you just give it to them instead of having them chase you around?"

She fiddled with her bottle. "I had planned on it. Even though Grandma wanted me to have it. I went to their office and overheard them talking, debating about killing me after they got it." She shook her head. "So why give it to them if they're going to kill me? I may as well keep it myself."

Protective instincts raged within him. How could someone do such a thing? He wanted to know Jeremy so he could kick the man's worthless ass.

"When I saw you continually looking at them, I thought you were part of their group." A gentle half smile. "Sorry."

Cale leaned back and rolled the bottle in his fingers. Those men hadn't been after her pendant. At least, not for the reasons she was thinking.

"And you've been running from them since France?"

"Those two are new. I've not seen them before, so from them? Yes. Much longer from my cousins."

"And you settle in Seattle, in this place."

"A while ago, I wouldn't have set foot in a place like this. I figure now, it's the best for me to be."

"Your grandmother was wealthy?" He sat forward and rested his arms upon his quads.

"Extremely. Which is why I don't understand why they want this so much. They got so much more in the will than I did. But I got this and they got pissed."

His palms itched and he fought the need to rub them on his thighs. "Can I see it?"

She rose and moved to sit on the coffee table before him, where she drew the pendant from her shirt. The gold shined against her mocha skin and he took a breath before touching it. Sparks exploded out, showering the room in a rainbow of color.

She fell back and scrambled from him. Eyes wide with fear and awe. "What the hell just happened?"

The lights danced around the room before choosing to land on her head and shoulders. As quickly as they'd arrived, they faded. His heart pounded out of control and from the way she had her hand on her chest, hers was acting the same way.

He knew what had just happened. She was his. The one made for him. Lian had told them all about it.

"One day you will find the one who is your other half. I can't tell you how you will know, just trust that you will. Embrace them. Cherish them. Protect them at all costs. For when the time comes, you will need their love to survive the tests you will face."

He was barely the legal drinking age and now he had a mate to protect. Need moved through him, but he ignored it, focusing on her face instead. Her brown eyes watched him as she struggled to sit up. He moved over her and offered a hand.

"No thanks. I'll get myself up."

"Are you injured?"

"Surprisingly, no. That was one hell of a shock." She pushed back up onto the chair she'd first occupied.

He wanted to touch the pendant again but had a feeling she wouldn't go for it. Not given what had just happened. "Let me check your neck. Make sure there's no marks."

Her laugh was a mix of humor and uncertainty. "No thanks. I'll look in the mirror."

Cale had to try. "I'd still like to see that pendant."

Her gaze narrowed slightly, but she leaned forward and drew it off, over her head. With obvious care, she placed it on the table before him. Quarter-sized, it lay there against a glossy magazine. He stared at the symbol and racked his brain, trying to remember where he'd seen it before. With care, he lifted it and turned it to the back. It was a labyrinth, he knew that, but where he'd seen one exactly like this, he couldn't quite recall.

Currents ran through his fingers and up his arm as he touched it. Taylor never took her gaze from his hand. As if she thought he might try to run off with the necklace. He didn't relinquish it when she reached for the chain. He wanted to see what would happen.

She hesitated but then she took the chain in her fingers. That rainbow of color surrounded her like an aura, pulsing with life. The pulses moving through him increased as well. If she noticed it, she didn't say a word, just took the necklace back and slipped it over her head, tucking the pendant once again behind her shirt.

"Do you know what the symbol is?" He picked up his drink to give him something to do with his hands.

"I remember my grandmother saying something about angels." A furrow appeared on her brow. "Seraphim, perhaps."

This time he knew she was lying. She knew exactly what it meant, she merely wasn't going to inform him. Not that he blamed her. She didn't trust him yet. That would change.

He nodded and sat back, ignoring every beat of his heart that told him to go to her. She was his now. And it was his right to claim her. Power shifted within him and he rolled his shoulders to calm down. It didn't do much, but he wasn't about to take her like an animal.

"Your cousins, then." He brought the conversation back to something he felt she would be more open to discussing. "Do you know where they are now?"

"Probably back at the mansion. Partying and having my grandmother turning over in her grave."

"Where's the mansion at?"

"South Carolina."

"You don't have a southern accent."

"I do, just tends to stick out, especially in a place like this. I work hard to hide it." A small shrug and she curled her feet beneath her and touched the chain.

It calmed her—the way she relaxed made it obvious. He didn't know what would calm him—his heart still hadn't slowed since that powerful shock between them. At times he could still see the rainbow of colors around her and it revved him up again. His tattoo shifted along his skin as his power answered his heightened stress.

Her phone rang, causing her to jump. "Excuse me."

Cale did his best not to eavesdrop while she spoke, but his hearing was just too good. Work had called her in—apparently someone last minute had reported as being sick.

"I'm sorry. I have to get ready for work. Also sorry about the misunderstanding before." She walked to the door.

Every fiber of his being told him not to leave her. She was in danger, even more than she could begin to fathom.

"I could wait and walk you to work," he offered.

"Give me five." She vanished down the hall and he heard the decisive closing of a door.

Whatever he'd activated by touching the pendant— the artifact he'd been tasked with finding—had only amplified the signal she would have put out naturally

Aliyah Burke

the closer the time came for him to find her. Problem was, not only he could see it. So he'd bet anything those two men were part of The New Order.

"*I found my mate.*" He sent the message to his siblings. And the congratulations rolled in.

"*When do we get to meet her?*" Aminta Tran asked.

"*Soon. Members of The New Order are after her. And that's not all. She has my artifact.*"

Tension could be felt through their connection. He was the first to have seen his, which meant the prophesy had begun to reach its zenith. Prior to his finding Taylor and the artifact, they had existed in a haze of almost ignorance, believing that so long as none of them had discovered it, they could train and pretend that perhaps the prophesy wasn't falling on them.

"*Bring her to the vineyard, Cale,*" Lian issued the order.

"*As soon as we can be there, we will.*"

"*Be safe, brother,*" Billy Kwan sent the sentiment.

"I'm ready if you are."

Taylor's voice pulled him roughly from contact. Wincing from the unexpected slivers of pain, he turned.

Jeans and a T-shirt, which told him whatever her job was, it didn't require business dress. She carried a black purse over one shoulder, nothing fancy, just plain and unadorned.

"Okay."

They walked down together and he tried to angle her toward his vehicle, but she shook her head.

"I walk. It's not far."

Senses alert, he fell into step with her. She was right—barely two blocks farther and she paused outside a restaurant.

"You work here?"

"I do. Thanks for the escort." She walked inside and disappeared without a look back.

Cale stood there for a moment before realizing he'd look foolish just staring into the building after her. So he went to a nearby bench and sat where he could see those entering and leaving. She may have thought that was the end of their association, but she was wrong. When she finished her shift, he would explain it all on the way to the vineyard.

* * * *

Taylor hefted the last bin of dishes into the sink to spray them off. As she worked, her mind drifted back to the handsome Cale Mattox.

That was some shock I got from touching him. Her entire body had lit up like a Christmas tree and she'd almost orgasmed right then. It had been hard not to let him touch her again, but she didn't think she'd be able to control herself a second time. So she'd opted to put herself back on the chair. Not have his assistance.

Even now, her body thrummed with mere anticipation of the next time he touched her. *Oh, grow up!* she reprimanded herself. *I left him outside this place. I'm not seeing him again.* Not that it wouldn't be nice, but she truly needed to be logical about this kind of thing. She had enough trouble with men in her life right now.

If he wants to kill me though, maybe he could do it through sex. She grinned at the thought. *Little death, hell. I'd want a big one.*

"Hey, Taylor."

"Gene. This is the last bit." She shut off the sprayer and moved the dishes to the rack where they would be sterilized.

"Thanks so much for coming in. I'm so glad you were available."

"No problem. Can always use the extra money."

"There's a guy out there waiting for you. Says he's a friend of yours."

Fear lanced through her, but she swiftly got it under control. "What's he look like?"

"Tall, muscled. White. Wearing a Grateful Dead shirt."

Her knees wobbled. Cale. *What is he doing here?* "Tell him I'll be out in a few."

"Never seen you bring a friend by."

She loved the concern she heard in Gene's voice. "He's from out of town." Glancing at her boss, she gave him a smile. "Thanks for looking out, Gene."

"Hey, you're one of my best workers." A shoulder shrug. "And I actually like you."

She laughed, well aware of how Gene sometimes came across as a blowhard. The two of them got along just fine, which was how she liked it. He was someone she could count as a friend.

Once the dishes had been pulled out to dry overnight, she finished wiping down the final counter, surveyed her job then grabbed her things. Pushing through the kitchen door, she spied him immediately. He sat by the door, leaning against the wall and appearing relaxed.

She wasn't buying it for a moment. In the low light, she swore she saw multi-colored sparks coming off him. It was as if she could see his restlessness.

Gene worked on his till and looked up at her when Cale rose. "All good, darlin'?"

"Set for the next shift, Gene."

"You two have a good night."

Cale walked to her side and smiled down at her. "We will," he stated confidently.

Outside, she turned to him and crossed her arms. "What the hell are you doing here?"

"We need to talk."

"Funny, that's basically what you said when you showed up at my door." She suddenly wasn't feeling so confident. It was dark and her body was telling her it was time to get out of there.

"That's because we're not done."

"Look, I've had a long day. Can we talk tomorrow? I can meet you somewhere for breakfast."

"I'm not leaving you alone." That statement was made with such finality she did a double take.

"Excuse me?"

His head shot up and he scanned the skies. "You heard me. We have to get you out of here. Come on." He set off and when she didn't immediately follow, he reached back and dragged her along with him.

It took her a few steps to get her feet back under her. Her skin tingled beneath his callused palm. "What's the rush?"

"Something wants you dead."

She jerked to a stop. He pivoted to glare down at her, displeasure evident. "Are you kidding me? I told you about my cousins and now you're trying to pull something like that?"

"I said some*thing* not some*one*."

She paused. So he had. That itch between her shoulder blades increased and she wanted to run home, lock her door and hide in the dark.

"Who wants me dead other than my cousins?"

Aliyah Burke

"It doesn't have a name other than evil." Another glance up. "We need to go, they're gaining."

"You don't know who but you know it's a they?"

"Demons usually travel together. Move." He began again at a jog and she stumbled along with him.

Demons. That was a new one. But since her senses screamed for her to get out of there and not necessarily away from him, she didn't fight or argue anymore. In fact, she picked up the pace. They thundered through the shadows to her apartment building where they went up the stairs to her place.

The instant they were there, Cale set about lowering and shutting all the shades and curtains. She locked all five locks on her door then went to help him. The bedroom as well was soon shrouded in darkness.

The glow of a single candle met her when she returned to the living room area. Cale's expression was serious and he fidgeted.

"What the hell is going on?"

He put a finger to his lips then beckoned her to his side. She went without argument, grateful when he draped an arm around her.

"Listen," he murmured in her ear.

It was hard to concentrate when her lust for him and his very touch raged out of control, but she did. She heard a soft flapping. "Like leathery wings."

"Demons."

She scoffed but swallowed her laughter when he covered her mouth with his hand. Surely he wasn't one who believed in that sort of lore. The flapping got louder, then came the scratching on glass. Her shivers increased one hundred times. She lived on the third story and there was something outside her windows. Trying to get in.

Mutterings floated along the air and she got cold. Clammy and even more scared. Cale blew out the candle and took her in his arms, lifting her and carrying her to the bathroom.

After the door clicked, he set her back on the floor but kept her close in his embrace.

"Why are we in here?" she whispered.

"Sometimes they can sense us through the windows. This room doesn't have any."

Not really a good job in cheering her up with that explanation. "Do you really..." She let it go, it wasn't the time to ask questions. Instead she wrapped her arms around him and pressed her face into his shirt. Lord, he smelled good.

They stayed in there for at least five minutes before he backed them out of there. Only then, he put her back in the room and started to shut her in alone.

"Stay here. I have to check to make sure they aren't inside waiting."

She gripped his shirt tighter. "No. I'm not waiting in here alone."

"Yes, you are. I won't risk you. I'll be back soon."

The kiss he laid on her was enough to stun her so he could close the door in her face. Short, demanding and possessive. That was how she would describe it. Oh, and perfect. She wanted more.

She sat on the tub's edge and tried not to scream when she heard thumping and scuffling out in her living area. A cry of pain had her at the door and bolting up the short hall. He might be unwilling to risk her, but she wasn't about to let him be killed or injured protecting her.

The sight she stumbled into gave her a moment's pause. *Maybe this is a movie. It sure seems like it should be one.* Grotesque creatures were in her living room.

Some with wings, some without. Scales, fangs and tails. *Yep, looks and sounds like a movie to me.*

However, and this was entirely unfortunate, the sounds they were making as they attacked Cale were all too real. Flames and lightning arced around the room. She wanted to run and hide, but she couldn't leave him alone. He fought five and she watched a sixth move around to land some hits from behind. And that was the one she focused on.

Hugging the wall, she inched her way along, stopping to grab the cast iron skillet she'd yet to put away. The heavy weight brought comfort. She swung it hard at the head of the thing watching and waiting for his shot. He crumpled like a ragdoll and she moved on to the next, swinging and cringing at the sounds that filled the room.

The silence, when it came, was deafening. Sweaty, she bent over and rested her hands on her knees, struggling for breath. Noxious odors stung her eyes and had them watering fiercely.

"I thought I told you to wait back there!" Cale thundered.

"What the hell is all this?" she retorted.

He gripped her upper arms gently, despite the ferocity in his expression. "You got hurt."

True, the things had nicked her a few times. But he bore more injuries than she did. "What about you? You're bleeding on my floor."

"I'll heal."

"So will I. But I still think these should be cleaned out. I'm guessing their nails weren't exactly sanitary." She turned and led the way back to the bathroom. "What the hell was all that? Things with wings, fangs, tails and I don't even want to know what the hell they were shooting from their mouths or hand-thingies."

Digging for the alcohol, she released him then pulled it out along with some wipes. Then went back in for the peroxide. In the mirror she caught sight of his expression. Angry. Dangerous. Sexy as hell.

"Not pleased with the disobeying."

"Yeah, I get that," she replied. She opened the alcohol and looked at the cut on her arm before pouring it over the cut. A sharp breath left her in a hiss. *Holy moldy shit! That hurts like a mother.*

"Are you crazy?" He grabbed the bottle from her.

Eyes streaming tears, she struggled again to breathe. Lord she wanted to curl up in a ball and cry. "I don't know what crap they had on them. I'm not looking to get sick."

"I could have healed you." He shook his head and pushed her so she sat on the counter. "Hold still."

"Not sure why you're sounding so exasperated," she muttered. "I didn't pour the shit on you."

Chapter Three

The chick was crazy. Cale strove for patience as he stared down at her. Even under the bright lights of the bathroom, she looked innocent and delectable. Her eyes shined from the tears she'd shed, but they were alert.

He couldn't believe it. Or wasn't sure if he should or not. She'd come out to help him. With a cast iron skillet no less. He was going to enjoy figuring her out. His own injuries burned, but he knew he had to ensure her safety first—his body would protect him.

The scratches on her shoulder worried him the most. The demon's claws had torn through her shirt and into flesh. He had to make sure they hadn't left anything behind in the wounds. The little bastards were good at doing such things.

"Take your shirt off. I need to check your shoulder."

"No way. Cut the sleeve and get access. I'm not undressing in front of you."

"We will see each other naked soon enough, Taylor. And as much as I'm looking forward to it, this is about your safety, not pleasure."

"Those lines work on other women?"

He furrowed his brow. "Other women?"

"Yes, do they? You know what, don't care. I'm not taking off my shirt. You can do it as I said, or I'll take care of it myself."

"You just dragged me down to this room with the intentions of cleaning injuries. Now you're shy?"

"I know you have a lot on your back you couldn't get. I was being helpful. Our own we could reach and they could have been cleaned by the individual but we could have shared the sink."

"You know you're ignoring the part where I said we'd be seeing each other naked soon enough."

She held his gaze and gave a grin he wasn't sure was kind. "I figured you're getting woozy from blood loss and just speaking out of your ass. So I decided it wasn't worth addressing."

He laughed and cut her sleeve so he had access to her injury. She was right—he could reach it this way. So perhaps he'd just wanted her shirt off. "I'm far from woozy. Hold still."

Cale could smell the stench left behind by the demon. They did it so if the person didn't die, they could find them again and either torture them or just play with them until they grew bored then killed them off. He focused on each tear and made sure nothing had been left behind. Then he pressed his lips to the corner—it wasn't necessary, but he wanted to—of the injury and allowed his power to seep into her.

He didn't move until the wounds had closed themselves. There would be a scar, but at least the poison and threat was gone. From that, anyway.

The colors were surging around her and they lit him from the inside out. Biting the inside of his cheek, he focused on the rest of her injuries. Then he stepped back, needing some space between them.

"What happened?" Her tone was low and full of awe. "It was like I could feel warmth flowing through me."

"Do you have any other places that they got you?"

"No. And I'm sure I don't need you to check for yourself."

"Such a shame. I would have loved inspecting you for some."

"Don't think I'm not noticing how you're trying to avoid my questions, Cale. But let me tend to your back. Then I'll press for answers."

He didn't need her to do anything, but he couldn't bring himself to step away. He wanted her hands on him, and if this was the way to do it at the moment, he'd take it. Cale shrugged out of his shirt, wincing slightly as the injuries pulled.

"Please don't dump alcohol on them." He offered her his back. "Peroxide is fine."

"How are you not collapsed in a pile on the floor with all of these?"

He didn't respond, for he didn't feel she was truly asking him, more making an observation. The smell of the hydrogen peroxide filled his nose and he sneezed. Then her touch came and he forgot, briefly, to breathe.

Her hands were warm and comforting as she poured then dabbed. "You know, I would suggest a hospital for this one" — she touched the long wound — "but I have a feeling that would just go in one ear and out the other."

It would. He glanced at his watch. They had to leave soon, for more would be coming. He didn't want to rush this, though. He'd felt so restless and unsure for so long. Her touch calmed all that and he wanted to luxuriate in it. Roll in it. Draw her close and crawl inside her where he could be surrounded by this feeling.

"There. Done."

He stepped away and stared at the ruined shirt in his hand. It didn't take him long to go to his bag and grab another. She was in the hall when he'd finished.

"So," she said, staring between him and the minor cuts on her arm, "how's about you tell me what all this mystical crap is that I'm suddenly involved in."

"We need to leave."

"Really? That's what you're opening with. I thought it may be more conducive if you told me about that thing you called a demon. The fire or lightning that came out of their mouths. But, sure. Let's start with we need to leave." She sat down and glared defiantly at him. "I'm not going anywhere. This is my home."

He bent over her, hands braced on the arms of her chair. "And those things know where you live. They *will* be back."

"Let me see. I didn't have them until you came into my life. So when you leave it, they'll be gone as well."

His tattoo shifted, a ripple along his skin, warning him time was running out. He knew there was probably a better way to break this to her but right now, he wanted her out of here and safe.

"They're after you, sweetheart, and that pendant around your neck. They won't stop, not ever, not until they get it in their scaly claws and drain your body of every last drop of blood."

That did it. Her skin paled as the blood rushed from her face. He wasn't, however, expecting what she did next. She kicked him square in the privates and he went down, swearing as stars flickered before his eyes.

Turning after her when she bolted for the door, he lunged to his feet as she jerked open her front door. Then screamed. He saw the demon. It reached for her, but she kicked him too. From the squeal of pain, she'd kicked him harder.

"Taylor!" he shouted.

She ran back to him, panic all over her face. Gathering her close, he went to her balcony then stepped out onto it. More were nearing and behind him he could hear that demon getting on his feet.

Tapping into his power, he jumped over the railing and down the three stories to the ground, her scream following them the entire way. He landed in a crouch, Taylor still in his arms, then he set her feet down as he rose. Linking their hands, he set off at a run.

When she pulled on his arm, he slowed.

"I can't go anymore," she wheezed. "Christ." She fanned her face and gasped a few times.

He watched her struggle to breathe and his concern mounted. "What's wrong?"

"What's wrong?" More wheezing. "What's *wrong*? You, you're what's wrong. You leap off a third story balcony, carrying me. Then take me on a five mile run."

"It was hardly a mile," he corrected.

"For someone who had asthma as a child, it feels more like five or ten. Damn it, I can't breathe."

Her chest rose and fell as she tried to calm down. Cale reached for her, but she smacked him away. He rumbled in his throat and grabbed her, pulling her tight to him. They stood near a streetlamp and he stared into her eyes. The fury in them made him proud—she was no wilting flower. She had more spunk than she knew.

Hands on either side of her face, he then repositioned one to rest upon her chest. He didn't like how fast it moved or how quickly her heart pounded. Still, she never took her gaze from his.

"Trust me," he murmured before reaching out and allowing their bond to further meld. *That's right, Taylor. Follow my heartbeat. My breathing.*

Soon her rhythms matched his and her color had come back to normal. "I don't have a clue what you did, but thank you."

One day he would explain it to her. Not presently, though. "Can you keep going?"

"Somehow I don't think I have a choice here."

He smiled at her. "Not really. Let's go."

His pace was a bit slower this time. He took them to a parking lot and hovered in the shadows while he searched.

"What are we doing here?"

"Getting a vehicle."

"I'm not even going to ask." She walked away, shaking her head.

Locating the one he wanted, he guided her with him. "They'll get it back, we just have to get out of the city."

"I meet you and suddenly can be charged with grand theft auto. Lovely." Her sarcasm wasn't lost on him.

He jumped in the Jeep, grateful there were no doors at all—one less thing he had to take care of—and began hotwiring it as she gingerly climbed into the passenger seat. It rumbled to life and he buckled his lap belt before shifting into gear.

"Oh look," she drolled humorlessly. "The list of things I don't want to know about Cale Mattox is getting longer with each passing second."

"It'll all be clear soon, Taylor."

"Of that I have no doubt. I see it now. A lovely eight by four cell with a small window for light. Some huge, mean cellmate named Bertha who wants me as her pet. Sexual pet, of course. Ah yes, my future is so bright." Exaggerated clapping. "Let's get this awesomeness started as soon as possible. Don't know how I can go much longer without Ms Bertha in my life."

He chuckled at her dramatic picture. "I won't let you go to jail."

"'Course you won't."

"Get some rest. I'll wake you when we get where we're going."

"Which is where, exactly?"

"A hotel. Out of the way so I can get some rest and heal up. Then we head home."

She huffed. "So glad we cleared *that* up."

Cale continued to drive, a smile on his face. The woman beside him was amazing. Of that there was no doubt.

* * * *

Taylor stirred and sat up. She lay on a bed covered by blankets. Hotel. She recalled Cale mentioning that. *Damn, damn, damn! I thought all that insanity was a dream. Or a nightmare.*

He'd left a light on near the bathroom, otherwise the room was dark with curtains drawn tight. She spied him lying on the other double bed that occupied their space. He was between her and the window.

Guess if something is coming in, it'll be through the window not the door. She went to the bathroom and took care of her pressing needs. Staring at her reflection in the mirror, she washed her hands.

What the hell kind of mess did I fall into? She thought about her past few hours since Cale had come back into her life. Demons. She shook her head.

"That is insane." She pointed at herself. "Don't you start buying into this demon crap." Canting her head to the side, she sighed. "Not sure how else to explain what I saw. Then there was the thing he did to this" — she stabbed her healed shoulder — "of which I have no logical explanation for either. And let's not forget whatever the hell it was that happened when he touched the pendant."

She hung her head and took several deep breaths before shutting off the light on her way out of the bathroom. With a glance to the door, she made her way back to the bed and crawled in. Unfortunately she wasn't tired. She wanted answers. Cale slept — he lay on his stomach and had one hand under a pillow.

"Wonder what he would do if I crawled into bed with him." The idea sounded so good. Much better than lying in this bed alone. She could really do with some contact right about now. Taylor kept to her own bed and just stared at his back.

When she saw some colors hovering around him, she frowned and peered closer. They flashed like sparks, giving the entire thing an appearance of pulsing. A wealth of colors, and when she reached out, they moved toward her, winding around her arm and sliding up to her shoulder.

"Wicked cool." It was, and she'd always been easily distracted by shiny things. This wasn't only shiny but also colorful and sparkly. Not to mention unlike anything she'd ever seen before.

It looked a bit different on her, for there was more gold in it. When it reached her neck, sparks—much larger sparks—shot out and filled the room, surprising her. Her scream woke Cale and she stared wide-eyed at the weapons in his hands.

"What?" He gazed around the room and the colors that were going off like fireworks.

"I think it's my turn to ask questions." She pulled her gaze from the display and focused on the man armed with some kind of sword. *Really? Who sleeps with that under their pillow?*

He sat opposite her and yawned before scrubbing a hand down his face. "I do owe you some answers."

"Yes, I think that's putting it mildly."

"Ask your questions, Taylor."

"What is going on?"

He pursed his lips and took a large breath. Sword beside him, he sat cross-legged on the mattress. "A battle for the world."

She moved her mouth a few times before anything would come out. "Battle for the world. Like, angels versus demons? You mentioned demons before."

"Good versus evil."

"Isn't that the same thing?"

"No."

She didn't like the sound of that. "So this isn't like some church thing of God versus the Devil then."

"No."

"But that was a demon. They," she amended. "They were demons."

"Yes. The ones that attacked were demons. The ones who were following you were members of The New Order."

She scooted to the edge of the bed and wrapped the comforter around her. "The New Order?"

"A group of fanatics who believe change is coming and they will do whatever they can to help it along. The change they want, however, is not...how do I say this? Beneficial to all mankind."

"I've never heard of them. What's their ideal?"

"Chaos. Darkness."

Chills broke out on her arms and she tightened her hold on the blanket. He sounded so serious and she couldn't pick up on any bit of joking from his end.

"How do they plan on getting to this point? I mean, you can't just shut off the sun. People aren't going to lie down and take it quietly."

"They are helping the ones who are fighting against those chosen to protect the world. Us, more specifically, the Astral Guardians."

That didn't sound good. *Really* didn't. With a gulp, she asked, "And who are the Astral Guardians?" *Yep, sounding more and more like a dream I truly want to wake up from.*

"My brethren and myself."

"But you're not an angel." *Why do I sound disappointed at that?*

"No angel." He held up a hand. "And before you ask, I'm not a demon either."

"Then what are you?"

"A warrior."

"Hence the weapons you sleep with," she muttered more to herself than him. Waving a hand, she wriggled her nose. "What does any of this have to do with me?"

"Quite a lot, actually."

She shook her head. "Nope, I don't want to know yet. Tell me more about you first. And your family."

"What you see with me is what you get, Taylor. I'm just like you."

She arched an eyebrow at him. "That I hardly believe. I don't sleep with swords and other weapons. I don't have sparkly colors floating around me. And what else?" She tapped her fingers on the blanket. "I know there was one more thing. Now, what was it? Oh yeah, I don't have demons chasing me."

"Actually, you do."

Head canted to the side, she asked, "I do what?"

"Have sparkly colors floating about you. The demon thing as well, for they are after you."

"Man, those colors are from you. Not me. They were moving around you." *I really don't want to address the demon thing. What the hell did I do to have demons chasing me?*

"They are only around me because of you."

That statement yanked her from her musings. "What?"

"They're like a beacon. They let your other half find you."

"My other half?"

"Yes. Unfortunately, the colors will also be able to be viewed by demons and other creatures of the dark, if they are also in the area and looking. Until you are actually in contact with your mate, the lights are a bit fainter."

She waved her hand around. "Do those look faint to you? Christ, I'll be able to be seen from the Space Needle."

"Yours are no longer faint. You've met your mate."

"Which I'm assuming is you." Her response was droll.

"Yes."

"And these lights are, what, just going around setting up arranged marriages? I mean, it's bad enough when parents want to do it, but now you're telling me some sparkly lights are responsible for setting me up with the man for my future? Forgive me if I don't buy into that craziness."

With her grand speech—without any screaming—over, Taylor felt proud of herself. She'd handled it like her grandmother would have wanted her to do. Stated herself well and hadn't given in to hysterics. Those, of course, were hanging around just waiting for her to slip.

"An arranged marriage? How do you figure?"

How could he not see it? "What were you doing in France?"

If he was taken aback by her change of direction, it didn't show. "I was skiing."

Right, she knew that. All this new stuff going on had pushed it out of her head. After all, skiing was inconsequential when you're running for your life from demons and who knows what else.

"So suppose someone walks up to you and says they were the one you'd been picked to marry. Spend the rest of your life with. How would you feel? What if you had a girlfriend?"

He canted his head slightly to the side, a furrow in his brow. "You're upset because you have a girlfriend? Are you a lesbian?"

Hysterics were getting even closer. She gripped the blanket tighter still. "No!" A deep breath. "No," she said in a calmer voice. "I'm not a lesbian. But for all you know, I could have a boyfriend. Now you show—"

His blue eyes went dark and she swore he had steam rising from his shoulders. Every inch of his body was rigid as he stared at her.

"You have a boyfriend?" Cale bit each word off and the room's temperature fell with every one of them. The warrior wasn't hard to see and she was impressed. His fingers flexed about the handle of the sword he still had in one hand. Yet, despite all that, she wasn't afraid. Not really.

"A second ago you thought I was a lesbian, now suddenly I have a boyfriend? Make up your mind."

He relaxed a fraction. "I never said I agreed you were a lesbian. I asked you if you were. And had you said no, I wouldn't have disagreed. Now, do you have a boyfriend?"

"No, but you're missing the point here. I could have and your lights would have lit my ass up for no reason. Who are they…? Maybe what are they would be better… Anyway, they have no right to tell me who I am supposed to be with."

He stood and stared down at her. The steam around his shoulders must have been a trick from the light, for she no longer saw it.

"Are you done?" he asked in a deceptively calm voice.

"Not hardly, but apparently you have something to say, so say it." *And here comes the flippant attitude Grandma told me to lose.*

He placed the sword on the bed he'd just vacated and stepped until he nudged her legs apart. Then he leaned forward, using his mass to push her back onto the mattress. When she stared up at him, heart pounding and palms sweating, he put his nose to hers.

"Your mate is not something you pick. We were destined for one another by the stars. Had you settled for someone else, you wouldn't be happy."

Those words set off trembling in both stomach and limbs. If only he meant them, as she wanted him to. She'd be lying if she said she didn't feel something more with him, something deeper than she'd ever felt with anyone else. Even men she'd slept with. This was more, so much more. Didn't stop her skepticism, though.

"You sure do have pretty words just to get my pendant."

Danger slashed across his expression and in his gaze. "If that was *all* I wanted, Taylor, I would take it. Make no mistake on that."

He kissed her. Not a quick one like what had happened between them in the bathroom of her apartment, either. No way. Lips connected, he slid his tongue into her mouth and she whimpered when he touched hers.

His taste was intoxicating. She opened further beneath his exploration and released her hold on the comforter in order to grip his shirt. Tugging him closer, she arched into him. In and out, his tongue stroked, and she closed her eyes as the colors around them flared even brighter.

Never had she wanted someone so much. She wrapped her legs around his waist and rocked against the hardness she encountered in his jeans. Yes, she wanted that. Wanted him. Wanted him deep inside her.

Bit by bit, he lowered his weight onto her and wound his arms around her, holding her tight. The kiss continued as he began flexing his hips, mimicking the motion of his tongue.

He lit her on fire and she wanted him to do whatever was necessary to quench it. Undulating beneath him, she conveyed her desire with actions, since he hadn't released her mouth. Damn man could kiss. He touched every part he could reach and continued to dance with her. Her pussy creamed and her breasts—pressed tight against his wide chest—

were almost painful with their need to be touched. Kissed. Caressed.

She was seconds from an orgasm when he pulled back. His gaze, a beautifully intense shade of zaffre, singed her. The blue hue was incredible and she wanted to dive in and see what awaited her.

"This is so much more than the pendant, Taylor. Never doubt that." Another breath-stealing kiss. "Ever."

Chapter Four

Cale stared at the woman lying beneath him on the mattress. The attraction between them was mutual. He wanted her, there was no doubt about that. However, her safety meant even more to him. He *had* to keep her safe.

Besides, their first time wasn't going to be in this rundown, roadside motel. Unless she continued to watch him with such passionate heat in her gaze. He was, after all, only a man. Astral Guardian or not, he was still a man. Brushing his lips against hers again, he pushed up and reluctantly left her body. She continued to lie there, all her curves tempting him. Her lips wet and slightly swollen from his kiss. A kiss he could have never stopped.

Instead of going back to the other bed, he sat near the headboard. After moving his sword to the table between the beds, he drew her up to curl into him, comforter and all.

"I need your help, Taylor."

She burrowed against him and humbled him with her trust. Being close during passion was one thing, but to do it after indicated trust.

"Why? Aren't you one of the Chosen...wait, what did you say you were called? Guardians? Astral Guardians."

The suspicion was blatant. "Yes. But I'm not invincible. None of us are."

"Right. Your brethren." She sniffed. "How many of them are you?"

"There are six of us right now who bear the marks."

"Marks?" She tugged the comforter up to her waist.

"Of our sign."

"Here's a thought, and keep in mind it's just that," she quipped. "If you want my help, maybe you should stop being so damn cryptic and just answer the damn questions."

Feisty. He liked that.

"I bear the sign of the dog."

Her sigh was heavy and she shifted against him. "Sign of the dog. Like Sirius?"

"Nope. From the Chinese zodiac."

"You're not Chinese."

He chuckled. "No, I'm not. And no, I wasn't born in the Year of the Dog." He rested his cheek against the top of her head. "It's different."

"How so?"

"We were picked by the animals and imbued with some of their traits and powers."

"This should sound so insane that I walk away right now, but given what I've gone through and seen in the past twenty-four hours, I'll give you the benefit of doubt. And I remember seeing an outline of a dog behind the design on your right shoulder when I cleaned your wounds."

"Yes, that's my mark. The dog image and the word in Chinese. Thank you for that, you know, giving me the benefit of doubt."

She harrumphed. "I know I'm going to regret asking this. Do you turn into this animal? I mean, I know very little about the Chinese zodiac, but I don't know how fair it would be for one to turn into a bunny and one a dragon. I mean, what if the dragon was hungry? No more bunny."

He chuckled. "No. We don't shift."

"Hence the sword?"

"Exactly. I've been training with weapons since I was fourteen."

"Are the others Chinese?"

"No. Some of my siblings are Asian, but again, it's not like that. This goes way beyond the simple labeling of something being in the zodiac. It started before people even had names for constellations, or the animals of the zodiac."

"You mentioned before good versus evil, but it wasn't an angels and demons kind of thing. Now you mention siblings — sorry, brethren — and training with weapons. Where the hell do you do something like that, and how are you chosen to be part of this? Then tell me how I got into it? I don't have any tattoo or mark. So why did your lights pick me?"

He could hear the stress in her tone, but it didn't overtake her questions.

"We live in Oregon. You'll see it soon enough. On a vineyard."

"So you drink all the time. Must help with the delusions you seem keen on having."

"Actually I don't drink at all. It's a home for troubled teens. We're taken in and taught how to work with others and behave in the world."

"So, this is like *X-Men*. A bunch of kids living in a mansion who train with their powers until the time comes to save the world."

Her analogies made him smile.

"I wouldn't quite go with that. We're not mutants for one. For another, we don't live in New York City. And not all the children there are Astral Guardians. And how do you know about the X-Men?" He rose and grabbed his bag before rejoining her on the bed. Digging through, he found a picture of the vineyard and showed it to her. "This is where we live."

"That's beautiful. I know a lot of movies. When you can't go out because people are hunting you, after a while there's not much to do inside other than watch television."

He hated that her own family was after her. "It's even more so beautiful in person."

"If this is such a battle, why would you have children who can't defend themselves there?"

"They don't attack there. I can't tell you why. I suspect it's part of their rules."

"Whose rules? Who's they?"

"*They* are the ones who want the world plunged back into darkness. I don't know their names. *They* are the ones who don't want us to succeed."

"Again? What, is The New Order going to blow up the sun? I mean, really? That wouldn't bode well for their survival either. The world isn't going to be plunged into darkness." She shook her head.

"I didn't mean literally, Taylor." *Although I can't be positive about that.* "I mean as in anarchy will reign. Evil will prevail and no one will be safe. Anywhere. Death and destruction will be the way life is lived. Daily. Kill or be killed."

"How do you know this?"

"The prophesy."

"You have a prophesy?"

"We have one."

"And it is what?"

"You really want to know?"

"I think so."

He could detect the hesitation but was proud she didn't run the other way. So he recited the prophesy to her, "*The parts to waken the world's hope have been scattered far and wide to the winds and throughout the stars. It is from there the chosen ones are marked, becoming Astral Guardians. Alone their individual defeat has a greater chance than when paired with the amaranthine and genuine love of their mate. Those Guardians must find, defend and bind the pieces to call forth the hope of the world. It will take courage, strength, love and sacrifice. If the Guardians fail, swift death will arrive to the one who calms the beasts. With this outcome, the world shall descend into darkness, chaos and anarchy.*"

"Not exactly cheerful," she mumbled.

Cale wasn't quite sure how to respond to that, for she was completely correct. It wasn't cheerful.

"Your brethren. Tell me about them."

"The two who've been there the longest are Tiarnán and Dracen. Then Billy. I came around the same time as Roz, and Aminta has been there the shortest amount of time."

"And they all have a mark of sorts." She crossed her arms and rested her head back on his shoulder. "So why wouldn't the...I'm not sure what to call them...things that sent the marks to you, match you up with each other? Wouldn't you be stronger like that?"

"The things that did that are beyond our scope of age, Taylor. This began back when the earth was born.

A battle for who would control it, and every so often the time comes to fight."

"I still don't know what I'm doing in the middle of all your craziness."

"You were chosen for me." He tipped her chin toward him as he told her that bit of information.

"So you say," she muttered.

"So *you* know."

He kissed her again and moaned deep into her mouth. When she tangled her tongue with his, he drew back. He wanted her so much, his cock was painfully hard. Instead of following his desire, he cupped her cheek and brushed a thumb along her skin. Such soft, smooth skin.

"We should get going," he said, refusing to release her gaze.

She shook her head as she climbed away from him and off the bed. "I must be absolutely insane for believing this, not to mention that I'm going along with it."

Cale watched her pace back and forth. The rainbow of colors had faded and only lingered in her hair. She was close to losing it, he knew that. And he understood it. This wasn't easy for anyone to accept. Add to it the running for her life, and he knew she had reached the end of her rope. Dark circles were prevalent under her eyes.

Strapping on his weapons, he continually peered up at her. She hadn't tried to leave the room and she wasn't cursing him. Bag in hand, he walked to her and the door.

"You can sleep more in the car."

"Whatever," she muttered, chewing on her thumbnail. She wouldn't look at him, just waited for him to open the door.

He did and stepped out first, keeping her inside. Senses alert, he searched for any lingering stench that accompanied those damn things. Nothing reached him, but he wasn't entirely sure there weren't members of The New Order out there waiting. Humans smelled like humans. He couldn't always distinguish good from The New Order.

They walked swiftly across the parking lot to where his stolen vehicle waited. As she climbed in, he continually checked the sky. Although the prime of the morning was still nearing, he didn't trust that the treetops didn't hold some creatures out to stop them.

He got them on their way and watched her from the corner of his eyes as she eventually slumped over and fell asleep. With each second he spent in her company, his protectiveness grew exponentially.

"We should be there by afternoon. I have to be careful, driving a stolen car." He sent the call out to his siblings.

"And your woman?" Roz posed the question.

"Currently sleeping. She's exhausted and wiped from everything that's happened. It hasn't helped she has been running from her cousins who want to kill her as well."

"I'll get a room ready for her. Or is she staying with you?"

"She can have her own room, Roz." Even as he sent the words, he wanted to growl in frustration. He wanted her in his room with him.

"Are either of you hurt?" Dracen asked.

"We got injured in the attack but I healed her, and by the time we get there, I should be fully healed. I need more shruiken though, I lost a bunch in those we fought."

"Travel safe, brother, and we'll see you when you get here."

"See you soon, Billy."

He was closest to Billy. They shared almost everything, and Cale would feel better when he was back surrounded by his friends and family.

Turning on some music, he kept it low so as not to disturb Taylor. He could see the chain that held her pendant clasped in her hand. It brought her strength — a blind man would be able to see that.

* * * *

She woke when they went over some bumps. Careful not to show she had awakened, Taylor snuck a glance through cracked lids. It was dark out and she couldn't make out much more than a parking lot and a few lights.

Cale parked them in an empty spot, in the back, then shut off the engine and killed the lights. She sat up.

"What are we doing here?"

"Waiting for a ride."

Her belly clenched, but she ignored the nervousness which grew. "From?"

"Billy."

She might be tired, but that name was familiar. Another of the Astral Guardians and a man he considered a brother. The knowledge helped to calm her a bit. *Right, unless you're being taken to a place for some kind of sadistic, freaky murder ritual thingy*, her subconscious chimed in with that most unwanted piece of news.

Keeping her head against the rest, she closed her eyes. Suddenly her life didn't seem so bad. Her old one. Running from those who wanted to kill her to running from others who wanted to as well. The ones she knew gave her a bit of an edge. These New Order psychos she knew nothing about. Nor the demons that were suddenly after her as well.

"Come on."

Cale got out, grabbed his bag then walked away.

"Don't bother waiting for me, or anything like that," she muttered. Following suit, she stepped from the interior only to run smack into Cale's chest. "Oomph."

She grabbed at him to keep from falling backwards. He slid a hand behind her, drawing her close to him.

"I'm not going anywhere without you."

"Tell me you can't read my mind." If he could, she was in so much trouble.

"Heard you muttering. Although with the way you say it, makes me wonder what kind of things you've been thinking about, Taylor Kenyon. And just how much they have to do with me." He leaned close and kissed the tip of her nose. "I can't wait to find out."

"I've not thought about you at all," she blatantly lied.

"Don't start lying now, sweetie. You talk in your sleep."

She'd forgotten that. And on the way here she'd had some lovely dreams of her and Cale in bed together. *Okay, so it wasn't just in bed. Shit, I really need help. On a massive scale.*

"I can't refute what may or *may not* have been said while I was asleep. For all I know, you're full of it and I didn't say anything."

"She knows you well. You have always been full of it." A new voice entered the conversation.

Taylor jumped and stifled her scream. Cale chuckled and that was all he did. *Must be Billy.* She loosened her grip on Cale and waited for him to do the same. He didn't.

"Billy." The man's name was said with affection.

A leanly muscled Asian man stepped into the small shaft of light there. His inky black hair had a rakish, messy look. The wide grin on his face immediately put her at ease.

Cale released her and the men embraced. None of that half-assed one-arm thing men tend to do when they're worried how showing affection will make them look. This told everyone of their affection, and it told her how deep it ran.

When they separated, both men glanced at her.

"Introduce us, Cale."

He didn't hesitate at the order. "Billy, this is Taylor Kenyon. Taylor, meet my brother, Billy Kwan."

She offered her hand, but Billy gave her a grin as he shook his head. "I'm getting a hug. And it's lovely to meet you, Taylor."

True to his word, he enveloped her in his embrace. Tentatively, she put her arms around him in return. Cale stood by watching with a matching grin on his face. Billy didn't keep her there long—there was nothing untoward about it. He smelled like the outdoors and a hint of spice. It was nice.

"I like her, Cale. Don't fuck this up. Come on, let's get home."

Billy walked away to the waiting SUV and hopped in the driver's seat. Cale guided her to the back and held the door while she climbed in. Before he shut the door on her, Cale leaned close and murmured, "Just so you know, I have no intentions of fucking this up, but I have every intention of fucking you."

She flushed and ducked her head. His chuckle lingered as he made his way to the passenger side to sit in front of her. Their soft chatter had her dozing off and on. The sun was just peeking over the horizon when they turned onto a road with a large sign that read *Tennesol Winery*.

Taylor sat up and stared out of the window. A thick mist covered the ground, but she could see the vines through it. Hills and flats added to the scenery. The majesty of it took her breath away.

Holy Hannah. This looks like something out of a magazine from Italy or France. She felt calmer the deeper onto the property they drove. Around a final corner and she stared at the house.

"It is so like the X-Men mansion," she said. "Or maybe Hogwarts."

"We're still not mutants," Cale replied. "Nor witches and wizards."

"Picky picky," she retorted.

Truth was, it wasn't like either. The estate was massive and gorgeous, however. *I feel for whoever has to clean this place.* She sat back and tried to absorb it all as they reached the door. Billy shut off the engine and got out, as did Cale. Taylor took her time before stepping out onto the drive.

The minute she closed her door behind her, the front one to the mansion opened and a man stepped through, his right hand curved about a cane. Middle-aged with a spot of gray at his temples, he too, was Asian. His race didn't bother her, what did was the way he watched her, as if he were assessing her. He carried himself with such presence, she felt overwhelmed. There was endless knowledge in his dark eyes.

"Cale," he said affectionately.

Cale went up the steps, taking them two at a time. The man's entire visage changed when the two embraced. She swore there was fatherly pride on his face. This man had to be one of the six. He seemed so strong and imposing.

And I've not said a word to him.

Together he and Cale walked down the steps, the man's gaze fixed upon her the entire time.

"Welcome, Taylor." A bow. "I am Lian Yang. It is my sincerest pleasure to finally meet you."

Drawing on her youth — growing up how she did — and the people she'd met then, she offered him a bow in return. "Thank you. It is also mine to meet you, Mr Yang."

A slight smile turned up the corner of his mouth. She laced her hands in front of her and waited. Cale moved back to stand next to her and she couldn't ignore the feeling in her that told her to lean against him. It told her how much she wanted him.

"Do come in. We will allow you to get settled then we must talk."

Mr Yang spun around and walked back up the steps he'd just come down.

I should have gone to him so he didn't have to walk them not once but twice. Disgusted with herself, she remained mute when Cale guided her up them as well.

The inside of the mansion took her breath away, as had the outside. Opulence was the name of the game here. And she'd thought her grandmother's home had been nice. While it had been, the fact remained it would have fit inside this place.

A coldness filled her as she recalled never being able to do anything in that house for fear of breaking some vase or knocking something over. She shook her head slightly. It would work, she wasn't about to go running through a house now. *Supposedly I've grown up and therefore won't be a danger to all these items, which look very expensive, or priceless.* How did the children here handle it?

"You're awfully quiet," Cale remarked as they walked up the curved stairs to the second floor.

"This place is huge. Do you ever get lost?"

"I did when I first arrived. Don't worry, it's not that bad. Plus, there are always kids around you can ask."

"Kids?" Okay, she had been beginning to wonder if the young ones were in a different building.

Cale nodded as they continued to another set of stairs onto the third floor. "He takes in troubled kids. Didn't I tell you that?"

"You said there were children, but I didn't know the place was like this at the time."

"What does that have to do with anything?"

"I wasn't allowed to do anything inside for fear of knocking something over and breaking it. And my grandmother's place looks poor compared to this. He's okay with them all running? What about his wife?"

Cale sobered. "His wife is no longer here, she passed a while ago. I never had the opportunity to meet her."

"Oh, I'm so sorry to hear that."

He brightened again. "They're kids. Accidents will happen. Not a lot of playing inside, though. There are plenty of acres around the house, stables for riding and so much more."

Sounded like Heaven.

"Here you go." He pushed open the door and allowed her to step through first.

Taylor stared in pleasure at what awaited her. Soft colors on the walls created a soothing feel. The queen-sized bed was piled high with pillows, the pastel green blending with ease to the other colors. The furniture itself was a dark gold hue. The window overlooked rolling hills and she even had a small balcony with a chaise longue on it.

"Beautiful," she said on a sigh. "Thank you."

He turned her toward him and tipped her chin up. The look in his eyes should have told her what was coming, but it still shook her anyway. His lips brushed against hers and she inhaled sharply as his tongue slipped along the seam of her mouth. Wanting what he had to offer and more, she opened beneath the slight touch.

Need hit her. Hard. She wound her arms around his neck and arched into him. Craving more contact with him, she pressed as close as she could get. He swallowed her moan as he lifted her and encouraged her to wrap her legs around his waist. Rocking against his hardness, she tried desperately to control the raging hormones coursing through her.

It didn't work—even her blood cried out for him. In and out he thrust his tongue, driving her closer to the precipice she desperately wanted to fall from. Suddenly he stopped and tore his mouth from hers.

Swiping her tongue along her lips to capture all his taste, she unhooked her legs from his waist. She held his gaze and didn't understand why he had ended the exchange between them. Perhaps things were different now that they were here.

In his eyes she could read his hunger and that appeased her a bit. He did want her, at least.

"There are clothes in the closet for you to wear. Your bathroom is over there as well." His words came out deep and raspy. Graveled.

Before she could say anything else, he whirled around and left her alone in the room. The slamming of the door jolted her, making her aware of the fact what they'd been doing hadn't been behind a closed door.

Body humming with a mix of frustrated desire and exhaustion, she showered then dressed in some clothing she found. Then she lay down on the mattress and moaned. After living how she had been, this bed was akin to Heaven. She closed her eyes, thinking of how it would be once Cale was in it with her.

Chapter Five

Cale practically kicked open the door to the room they gathered in for planning. *Danger room.* Taylor's words popped in his head. A slight smile graced his lips momentarily before he wiped it clear.

"What was the smile for? You seemed like you wanted to kill me when I called you." Billy smacked him on the shoulder as he passed by and took his typical seat.

"Just thinking about Taylor thinking we're like the X-Men. She'd probably think of this as part of the Danger Room." He sat. "And yes, I did want to kill you for calling me. Still do."

It had been hell letting her out of his arms. He really should have told them he'd be there in ten and ripped her clothes off. Taken her against the wall. The door. Anywhere, just so long as he was allowed to be buried deep inside her.

His cock throbbed and he shifted in the seat, searching for a more comfortable position. It wasn't easy to find one.

"So, what's the urgency?" he asked, wanting to get back to Taylor.

Tiarnán and Lian entered the room seconds later. Cale stared at the oldest Guardian. No smile on his face — Tiarnán didn't have much of a sense of humor. His thick black hair hung free around his shoulders and he had dressed in his typical attire of jeans, cowboy boots and a plain white shirt. His loose-limbed gait had a way of throwing off his opponents. The man was the fiercest warrior of them all, although Dracen was a close second.

"Good to see you." Tiarnán sat after his welcome.

"You too, man." He directed his attention back to Lian, who took his seat at the head of the table.

"I am sorry, Cale, for pulling you from your guest. I need everyone to be extra vigilant."

His tattoo moved, rippling along his skin. The flare of power in the room suggested the others' had as well.

"What's going on?" he asked, suddenly alert.

"I've seen marks around the property which lead back to those who want our destruction. So they are starting to creep closer."

"Is this because of me finding the artifact? And Taylor?"

Lian shook his head. "I can't answer that. Sometimes they know before we do. All we can do is prepare the best we can and be ready."

Cale didn't like that answer. Crossing his arms, he asked, "Where are the others?"

"Aminta got called back to service. Roz is gone for a while as well. Dracen is out picking up three more children who will be staying here," Billy said.

He nodded. "Taylor doesn't believe what I've told her. Hell, she doesn't believe what she's seeing with her own eyes."

Lian stared at him. "She will come to terms with it when she's ready. She has been through a lot lately, being on the run from those she should be able to trust. Give her some time."

"We don't have time if they're sniffing about," Cale bit off.

Lian lifted his brows and gave him a look he'd not seen since he'd first gotten here. Immediately he snapped his mouth shut.

"If she isn't ready, it won't matter anyway. You need to learn patience, Cale Mattox. You are always going, never slowing down. Learn what it is to do nothing and allow what you seek to come to you."

What the hell does that mean? Instead of voicing his question aloud, he nodded.

Lian continued to talk, and Cale focused the best he could. Honestly though, he was having a hard time. All he could see was Taylor and that pale green bedspread. How would she look sprawled naked upon it for him to enjoy? He would start at one end and work his way to the other, turn her over and work back. Then start all over again.

"Pay attention."

Damn it. His cock was painfully hard and he'd lost the conversation. "Can this wait until Taylor is here? I think she should hear it as well."

Lian narrowed his gaze slightly. "Why is that?"

"This has as much to do with her as it does any of us. Why would I want to keep her in the dark on it?"

"You care greatly for this woman."

Staring at the man who'd taken him in and given him a home, he shrugged. "I respect her and what she's gone through. She's smart and determined. Good traits. She is one of the strongest people I've met. Having gone from a pampered life to running for her life and making it. Through it all, she keeps her sense of humor."

The three of them stared at him, waiting for him to admit it. He knew that. They knew he knew that.

"Yes," he conceded. "I care for her." He didn't want to give them everything they wanted.

Billy grinned. "Glad to hear it. I think this woman is going to give you a run for your money, bro."

"Why?"

"She's not going to buy into your little adventurous travel dude attitude you like to have. No more picking up and running off to the slopes or beach now."

He snorted and rolled his eyes. Cale was the youngest of the male Chosen and they loved to pick on him. He didn't want to admit that Billy was right and he would have to curb that behavior. Unless he could convince her to go with him.

No, it wouldn't do to have her in trouble. And if she went out with that pendant on, it would act like a homing beacon to the other side. There would not only be demons and the like, but also members of The New Order hunting them down.

And he was not going to put her in harm's way. Rocking back in his chair, he glared at Billy. "Plenty to do here."

"I'm sure. But you have to leave the bedroom at some point."

He flipped Billy off and turned his back on him. It did him good to see a slight grin playing on Tiarnán's lips. Even Lian had a smile, but Cale could detect the sadness in his.

"Back to business," Tiarnán said, picking up a remote and turning on the screen along the back wall.

* * * *

Sore and tired, Cale made his way up to his room. Normally he could hold his own, but today had been all about getting his ass kicked. Tiarnán hadn't had any sympathy for him either. In fact, if anything, he'd seemed to push him harder.

After training, they'd gone to see the new weapons that had been made, and Cale had to admit, he'd liked that part. He'd picked out a few he would try next time. He fought another yawn and rubbed his eyes.

A shower. That will help.

Pushing open the door, he stripped as he walked across the room, making a beeline to the shower. He didn't linger too long—the water didn't revive him as he'd hoped it would. After he'd finished, he stepped from the walk-in and wrapped a towel around his waist once he'd used it to blot the majority of water from his skin.

He yawned again and walked back out to the bedroom where he paused. Taylor lay on the bed, sound asleep.

How'd she get into my room?

It took him a few moments for the reality of what faced him to sink in. She wasn't in his room, *he* was in *hers.* He took in the pale green covers and realized he'd come straight here following training.

Glancing down, he blinked a couple of times at the pastel pink towel that hung low on his hips. *Not really my color.* He flicked his gaze between himself and where she lay curled up on her left side, facing away from the door. It was as if she'd fallen asleep in the act of crawling into bed, too tired to even pull the comforter and sheet over her.

The sun, which streamed in through the window, glinted off her hair and skin. Her hands rested beneath her chin as she slept. Cale took another glance around the room then approached the bed. He slipped in behind her and covered them with the blankets.

Moving slowly, he spooned her, one arm draped around her midsection. She never stirred and he couldn't sense any difference in her breathing that would indicate she'd woken but was trying to pretend otherwise. Her soft hair brushed the underside of his chin and he took a deep breath, inhaling the gentle scent that wafted from her. Then he closed his eyes.

Someone was in bed with her. Taylor alternated between panic and more panic. Mostly because for some reason, the person with her brought her a sense of calm and comfort. Along with arousal.

Cale.

After she'd calmed herself down a bit and thought about it, she realized who it was. *What is he doing in my bed? Perhaps we were expected to share a room and bed.* That hadn't been cleared with her, but then, hey, not much of this most recent stuff had. Her belly, tight with nerves, kept encouraging her to bolt and go somewhere else. Anywhere. Get away from him. Keep a distance, for he could only hurt her. A sentiment her brain agreed completely with.

Her heart was another story entirely. She closed her eyes, blocking out the view out the window. *Am I seriously thinking there is, or could be, something with me and this man? I can't be that foolish.*

Apparently she was, for her heart wanted to trust and believe in him. He'd kept her safe, saved her, and right this very moment was holding her as if she were precious to him. At least that was what she felt with his arms around her, as they were currently.

It's official. I can't trust myself. It's merely me being grateful for him helping me. I don't know him enough to have any kind of feelings for him.

Someone knocked on the door and she wanted to hide under the bed. *Oh, my God. What are they going to think if they find him here in bed with me?*

The knock came again. She didn't move. Perhaps they would just go away. Did her luck hold out like that? Of course not. Cale stirred and climbed from bed, mattress dipping as he left. Everything in her wanted to turn and watch him walk to the door, but she remained facing the window.

"Yeah?" His voice was deep and sleep-roughened.

The nerves in her belly were of a different kind now. Taylor tightened her legs and did her best to ignore the longing moving through her. She couldn't act like a slut. There was too much at stake.

"Oh," a woman said. "I didn't mean to...interrupt. I came to see if Taylor would like to go shopping for some clothing. I know she didn't have time to get a lot of her things."

More like no time to get any of my things. Not that I had much, but still.

"I'm sure she'd like that. I'll send her down to meet you."

"Great. Good to see you back, Cale."

His response was muffled before the click of the door reached her. He made no sound as he moved across the carpet, but she couldn't miss the man who stood before her wearing nothing more than a pink towel. She'd been staring out from beneath lowered lids and it took everything inside her not to allow her eyes to fly open.

He had no right to look that good in pink. Seriously. The six pack was more like an eight and she couldn't spy an ounce of fat on him. Her mouth dried as she took in the view best she could without giving away that she was awake.

"How long are you going to pretend you don't see me standing here in this pink towel?"

"As long as it takes for you to move."

"So you are awake?"

Why did it sound like he was enjoying this?

Maybe I should be asking myself why it is I want to unwrap the towel and see what lies beneath. Like that would be a good thing to do. Nope, she had no intention of doing that.

"Of course I am," she snapped. "Someone was knocking at the door."

He tugged on the blanket and she jerked her gaze up to his face, determined not to focus on anything else with wide-open eyes. But, Lord, that temptation was there to leisurely drag her gaze up and see it so much clearer.

"Why are you in my room?" she asked when their eyes met.

"I was tired and wanted to see you."

She shook her head. "That doesn't make any sense. If you were tired, you wouldn't be seeing me because you'd be sleeping. Try again."

Her breathing hitched when his towel shifted down, showing off more of that tanned skin. Christ, what did he do? Sunbathe in the nude? Shouldn't his skin be a bit paler down there?

"All right, I just came here after training. Took my shower and came out here to find you lying there asleep. I joined you."

More slippage and she wanted to shift against the sheet, but she held herself still. If he wasn't going to bring attention to it, she wasn't going to say a thing. *Because you want to see what he looks like. How long his cock is and how thick.*

Damn her subconscious.

Struggling to keep her focus on the question she had, she licked her lips. "So we're not sharing a room?" *Did I sound disappointed by that?*

"Do you want to?"

Oh, he just had way too much sexual appeal for her. She was out of her league. Swallowing back the *yes* that dangled on the tip of her tongue, she shook her head. "No thanks. I just wasn't sure if we were because you brought me here. And there's all that prophesy stuff. I'm sure we could get a cot or something, if we were."

His laughter had the towel almost falling off. She was torn between telling him to fix it and giving it the final little jolt needed for it to settle on the floor.

I am not a slave to my desires, I can ignore this. Yeah right. She'd never wanted anyone more. Her body ached with the need for his touch and ignoring that wasn't easy in the least.

"Babe, if we're sharing a room, we're sharing a bed." He stepped closer until his legs touched the mattress' edge. "I'd not be on a cot while you lay in a bed feet away from me."

"I would take the cot."

"No. You wouldn't. We'd be together. Naked. Limbs entwined." The mattress dipped as he placed his right knee on it. "My tongue exploring every inch of your soft skin."

She whimpered in the back of her throat. From the flare of heat in his gaze, he'd heard her. He put one hand by her shoulder and leaned close.

"My cock, thrusting into your wet pussy. Over and over until our cries blend as one. I want to feel you come around me. I want your nails digging into my back as I fuck you. I want to lay there while you ride me."

He straddled her as she lay on her back, his dark hair falling around them. Her entire body trembled at the picture he painted. She wanted that, too. Now. Biting the inside of her lower lip, she fought the urge to buck her hips up into him. She heard the whisper of the towel sliding free and she knew he was buck naked.

"I thought I was supposed to go shopping." *When did my voice get so breathless?*

He bent his arms and brought himself closer to her face. Turning his head at the last moment, he placed light, teasing kisses all over her cheeks and neck. Nose as well, he just avoided her lips.

Her body was strung tight and craved release. Soon. Before she burst into flames.

"Touch me, Taylor."

Those three words flowed on a thread of begging and command. She couldn't hold out any longer. Biting her lower lip, she lifted her hands and placed them flat upon his bare chest which was close to hers. His skin was warm and she shivered at the pulses that traveled through her at the contact.

"Yes," he groaned, lowering his hips.

His thick cock rested against her core and she shifted as she tried to widen her legs. Desperate to have him

closer still to be able to wrap her limbs around him.
He readjusted and she hooked her ankles about him.
A faint humming grew in her ears, but she didn't care.
Nothing was going to stop her now. She wanted him.
He wanted her. If there were going to be regrets, they
would happen later.

"Much later," she muttered.

"Much later what?"

She shook her head, not wanting to address her
thoughts. "Kiss me."

"Thought you'd never ask."

And he did. Lord, did he. His tongue thrust hungrily
through her mouth as he rocked his shaft against the
seam of her pants.

In between kisses that curled her toes and damn
near delivered her to orgasm, he stripped her of all
clothing. In the back of her mind, she longed to
explore him but right now, it was about taking the
edge off her need. His need. *Their* need.

He made love to her breasts. The tips beaded tight
and with every rasp of his tongue, nip or suck on them
she squirmed beneath him. She undulated, trying to
get his length where she craved it most. Inside her.

"Tell me," he murmured against her breast before he
grazed the sensitive point with his teeth.

"You…in…me…"

"Tell me to fuck you, Taylor. Tell me the words I
want to hear and I'll do it."

She tried to argue with him, but her body rebelled
against her. It wanted what he had for her. Digging
her nails into his shoulders, she leaned forward and
nipped at his pectoral.

"Fuck me, Cale. Fuck me."

The rumble came from deep within his chest. She
felt as much as heard it as the sound rolled through

her. In one swift stroke, he sank fully inside her. She gasped at the feeling and shook from the orgasm that blindsided her. He didn't give her a chance to get used to him, he just began to move.

"So fucking tight," he uttered in her ear.

Cale pounded his cock into her over and over again as she rose and fell in time with his strokes. Legs high about his waist, she purred in pleasure when he rolled his hips and slammed in again, repeatedly.

She closed her eyes and hung on for the ride. It was rough. It was incredible. It was just what she needed. This wasn't about words of love or tenderness. This was intense and fierce.

Another orgasm overtook her and she cried out. He pulled back, slipped his hands to her waist and lifted her. Nose to nose again, he began all over and she trembled, her body not used to this type of passion. The all-consuming kind, and it had consumed her — totally.

She burrowed her face into the side of his neck and rocked with him as he changed speed and slowed. He felt so good inside her and amazing around her. She didn't want to leave. Their sweat and the scent of sex filled the air.

"Come for me again," he demanded in her ear.

"Can't," she whimpered, body trembling with exhaustion.

"Yes. Once more."

He took them off the bed and carried her to the shower, remaining deep inside her, each step impaling her farther on him. Soon they stood in the shower, warm water cascading around them and the tiles against her back.

Cale positioned them so the streaming water hit her belly. She watched him. His eyes burned possessively and she liked how it made her feel. Wanted. Desired. His.

"Once more, Taylor."

Her hands were on his forearms and he continued to stroke endlessly inside her. She'd lost count of how many times she'd come on his cock, but she didn't think there was anything left in her.

His hands moved over her body and, combined with the water, they brought her back to a hypersensitive state. He held her gaze as he moved one hand to her pussy and exposed her clit to the water. She gasped and tightened her grip on his waist with her legs.

"Cale!"

He readjusted her a bit more so the stream was directly on her. His thrusts grew more demanding and she closed her eyes again as the orgasm he'd demanded from her rushed over her. Back arching, legs gripping, internal muscles tightening around him...she screamed as she came. His roar joined her cry as his release pulsed up into her, filling her. If this was how she was to die, sign her up—she was on board.

Chapter Six

Cale leaned against the pillar and watched Taylor interact with some of the children who'd been brought here. Even now, from this distance, all he could think about was the feel of her tight pussy around his cock. He wanted her again. And again.

He'd not seen her for a few hours after she left his arms. Dracen had taken her shopping and they'd come back in time for dinner. Now she was spending time with the children.

Movement at his elbow had him spying Dracen stopping beside him. He might be taller than she was, but she was like a mother to him. Mother and sister.

"Thanks for taking her shopping."

"I had some other things to pick up in town. Besides, I think it did her some good. Hard for anyone to be stripped of everything you know."

He thought about that damn purple bag she'd always had with her. They'd not even been able to bring that. "It's been a rough few days for her."

"I'd say not only her."

"I don't have a choice—I'm one of the Guardians."

"Still doesn't mean it can't be rough for you."

He put his gaze back on Taylor. She wore jeans and a long sleeved shirt as they played ball outside in the cool evening. "Where are Roz and Aminta? Aren't they coming back soon?"

"Doesn't look like it. From what it sounds like, they have found their artefacts as well."

"So that's three of us. Or have you sensed yours?"

"Nope, nothing here. Tiarnán hasn't either. Not sure about Billy."

He could hear the frustration in her tone. "Do we know any more of what's supposed to happen?"

"No. Lian is being more tight-lipped than usual and he's not even giving riddles. It's odd, I don't know what to make of it."

"All we can do is be alert. And kick ass when the time comes."

Dracen rubbed her upper arms. "Yeah, something like that."

No disguising her disbelief and worry. He wrapped an arm around her waist and brushed his lips along her temple. "Lian's trained us well, Dracen."

"I know. I'm just not sure. I mean, if all of us sense the artefacts at the same time, how can we be there for one another?"

"We can go to them if they need us." It disturbed him how nervous this was making her—Dracen rarely got flustered. "Taylor is here and safe. The others will be fine as well."

Taylor began heading their way. Dracen pasted a smile on her face and nodded. "You're right." She had composed herself by the time Taylor joined them. "You work well with children, Taylor. And it's obvious they enjoy you."

"Thank you. I like them." She moved her gaze between him and Dracen. "Am I interrupting?"

"Heavens, no. I was just saying hi to him. I'm off to get a few things done. If I don't see you again before tomorrow, have a great night." With a wave, Dracen walked away.

Taylor looked at him. "Are you sure I didn't interrupt anything?"

He bent his head and pressed their mouths together. His body roared in response, but he kept his arousal in check. "Positive. Come on."

"Where are we going?"

"To see Tiarnán and Billy."

"Right, Wolvie and Gambit."

He paused and shook his head. "What?"

"Well, Tiarnán is so serious, he is like Wolverine. And Billy is light-hearted and a flirt. Like Gambit. Or Iceman."

"We're not mutants."

"Right. Powers, big mansion, evil fighting you. I can't imagine why I keep making that comparison."

"Come on, woman."

He was glad she wasn't freaking out about what had happened between them. Especially when he'd thought she would at least try to avoid him after. He hadn't been sure how their sleeping together would have been taken. Quite the opposite.

She walked beside him as he led them through the mansion. Her amazement was infectious. He found himself smiling along with her as she took in the decor and other things lying around. Things he'd not really paid any attention to—they were just part of the house. But Taylor was impressed. Not with the money spent on the items, but on the items themselves.

"What is it about this stuff that you like so much?" he asked as she stood beside a Ming vase.

"Really? Think about it. Back in a hard time, one most of us now wouldn't survive in, they were creating such works of beauty. We have all this technology now and it's a machine that does it. These were made by hand, painted by hand. I mean, how did they make the colors? The porcelain?" She shrugged. "It's so interesting to me to see how now, with all our so-called advances, we don't seem to create such beauty. Not without putting it in a computer and having a machine do it for us."

"Do you have an ancient art degree?"

"God no. I didn't go to college. My grandmother didn't think it would be necessary for me to do so. I had money, well she did, and she figured I'd marry money. No sense in filling my head with nonsense learning from books."

"Feel free to use the library as much as you like. And I'm sure Lian would love to talk with you about some of the items here."

Her smile brightened his soul. "Thank you."

Swiping his finger along her cheek, he responded in kind. Then continued on the way to their destination. He pushed open the door and waved her in before him. They were the last to arrive.

"Danger room," she whispered.

He tried not to laugh. It was what he'd thought she'd think of it as.

"Finally, something beautiful to look at," Billy said with a grin. "No offense, Tiarnán, but you just don't do it for me."

Tiarnán blinked hazel eyes. "Crushed." He turned an unemotional gaze toward the two of them.

"Sit down, Taylor." Cale put her in the seat beside him. The one Aminta normally occupied.

"Can we see it?" Billy asked.

"We need the pendant, Taylor." Cale touched her arm.

Instantly her calm vanished and she tensed. "Why?"

"To see if we can get anything from it which may give us hints on where the others are. Or what they are."

Her reluctance saturated the room. Rubbing her skin with his thumb, he frowned over the speed of her pulse. "I didn't think you'd let me take it without you so we figured it would be better this way. It won't leave this room without you, Taylor. Just let us take a look at it." He tried to cajole her but knew she wasn't completely on board.

"The necklace will stay here in the room," she said, more to herself than anyone else.

A zipping sound reached them as she skated the pendant along the filigree chain. He could see the other two relax with relief when she removed it from her neck and coiled it in his hand.

As before, sparks exploded throughout the room when they both touched it. Taylor wouldn't meet his gaze—she wouldn't take hers off the item he held. Billy and Tiarnán murmured under their breath and watched the display.

"Is that common?" Tiarnán asked.

"Every time the both of us touch it, yes."

"Hand it over," the eldest demanded.

Cale did and watched as Tiarnán stared at it, flipping it over in his hand. Then he set it down on a metal plate on the desk and pressed some buttons.

The screens on the far wall lit and a pale blue light shot up around the necklace. Three dimensional images of the item showed on the screens, different angles and views.

"What is that?" Taylor's question was full of awe.

"Computer," he said. He pushed his chair back and went to the middle one. "Enlarge this one, T." He pointed at the frontal vision of the pendant with all its symbols and markings.

She'd never seen anything like this before, except in the movies. If something from one of those science fiction or paranormal movies had ever come to pass, this was it. In spades. Taylor watched her grandmother's pendant hovering in the air, the blue light surrounding it and projecting numerous views of it on the many screens.

Part of her wanted to snap it away from them and return it to where it belonged. Around her neck. The stronger urge, however, was the one to see what all this stuff could do.

X-Men, hell. This is like Iron Man, and who knows what else. Batman. The Batcave probably had this kind of shit going on in there.

Her eyes drifted back to Cale, where he now stood in front of one screen. Tiarnán had risen to his side and they stood talking softly between one another. Billy seemed interested in another image.

Tiarnán scared her, if she wanted to admit it to herself. Hell, even if she didn't want to admit it. He did. It wasn't like she was worried he would do something to hurt her. Not at all. He was just so intense and serious. She knew if what they said was true and all this was coming down the pipe, he would protect her, but she doubted he even liked her.

A good looking man for sure, with his thick black hair and hazel eyes. Well-muscled and if a woman wanted a man who looked like he'd just strolled off a ranch or the back of a horse, well, he was the one. She'd thought Cale was a good size, but as they stood now, side by side, she realized that Tiarnán was much bigger. Still, both men were without body fat. She couldn't say that about herself.

Billy was the leanest of the three. He was built more like a runner, with wiry muscles. Tiarnán was taller than Cale and Billy as well. She liked Billy—he made her smile and feel at ease, quite the opposite of Tiarnán. Billy caught her looking at him and gave her a wink and a grin.

"Come here," Billy said with a wave.

She pushed back the chair and it rolled soundlessly over the carpeted floor. Taking her time, she made her way down to where Billy waited for her, gesturing to the seat beside him.

"Look at this."

Hell, they had a small monitor built into the tabletop, which had his attention. She sat, grateful for the comfort of the chair.

"Zero gravity."

"What?"

"The chairs. They're zero gravity, which is why they feel so nice. I heard your groan when you sat."

What was she supposed to say to that? She gave him a slight smile. "What are you looking at?"

"The chain."

"Why?"

"Because it's not just a filigree. Look here."

He pressed some buttons and up popped a 3D image right between them. The entire length of the chain was there, like someone was holding it in a circle so they could look at it from all sides.

"Incredible."

"Look closer." He blew up the image and stretched it out even more.

Taylor frowned as she stared at it. "Wait, are those symbols that make up the chain?"

"Yes."

"I never noticed." She reached out toward it only to pause. Billy took her wrist and put her hand into the image. She could touch, turn and maneuver it. "Wicked," she breathed.

The filigree chain was gold, like the pendant. Inside each oval, seemed to be a collection of Asian characters. She didn't know what language, but she'd seen enough on tattoos and things like that.

"What is this?" she asked him, turning the chain to see more.

"It's Chinese. Guys, you're gonna want to see this."

Tiarnán and Cale appeared and she felt Cale's hard leg next to her against her side when he leaned over.

"Damn," Cale said. He put his hand on her shoulder and gave a gentle squeeze. "It's all the animals in the Asian zodiac, as well as the words for the others. And more."

"Like you wear on your shoulder?" she asked Cale.

His long fingers joined hers in the image, spun it around to a specific one then touched it before scaling it larger. "This is mine. The dog."

She stared at it and scanned the rest of the chain. The same symbol was there a few more times. While it was gorgeous, it was also freaking her out a bit. Why hadn't she noticed this before? *Like back when I got the thing from my grandmother.*

"I swear I don't recall seeing those markings on it before. The pendant, yes but not on the chain. It was just a smooth filigree."

"Maybe when the sparks happened?" Tiarnán suggested. "That was a big display you put on here just now."

"Smaller than the first time," Cale commented, dragging his fingers along the back of her neck.

She blushed and wanted to hide. Yes, what he said was true. *But it's* how *he said it. He doesn't have to make it sound so, well, sexual.* Even so, she still wanted to smile. For a few seconds, she allowed herself to think about what it had been like to be in his arms.

"It would make sense," she said ignoring his comment. "I've not really looked at it since he touched it the first time." A slight pause. "Well, makes sense as much as any of it can."

Cale reached out and took the necklace from where it hovered above that metal plate then draped it over her head. Instead of moving away as she'd thought he would, he remained behind her, hands upon her shoulders, rubbing lightly. Normally the display of public affection would sit a bit at odds with her, but right now, she needed it.

"There are a few on here that I'll have the computer pull up. My Chinese isn't all that impressive, sorry to say." Billy shrugged and began typing.

"What about the pendant?" she asked, refusing to be cut out of whatever it was they were trying to get to the bottom of.

"One of the symbols on the back is hope," Cale said. "The second, I'm not sure and I don't entirely know what the markings along the front side are, but the computer should find it out in no time. We'll give the stuff to Edmond, he'll figure it out for us."

"Did your grandmother give you anything else?" Tiarnán posed the question.

"Nothing like the necklace. I mean, money of course from the will, the necklace and, oh, the purple suitcase." *Who's Edmond?*

"That leopard-print catastrophe?" Cale sounded shocked.

"Yes. She gave it to me about a month before her death. I was shocked, given how she'd always been about appearance, but she just smiled and said sometimes a woman has to do something outrageous. I chalked it up to her one outrageous thing."

The three men stared at each other. "I have to go back and get it," Cale said as the others commented on how he had to go.

She glanced at him. "When do we leave?"

"Sorry, honey, I'm not taking you with me." Cale shared a look with Tiarnán, and Taylor frowned when she saw a fog or mist rising from his shoulders.

"What do you mean you're not taking me with you? You're leaving me here?"

"Yes. Billy is here, along with Dracen, Lian and the others. Tiarnán and I will be handling this."

She glared in his direction and pushed away with her legs. The chair rolled smoothly beneath her command and she crossed her arms when he arched an eyebrow at her.

"What?" He checked his watch. "I have to get going."

She was so furious she didn't even know where to begin. So she didn't. Stuffing the pendant down her shirt, she jumped to her feet and stomped to the door.

"Taylor!"

She ignored him and left the room, slamming the door behind her. How dare he? How dare he leave her behind? Hell, if it wasn't for her he wouldn't have the precious pendant.

"Artifact," she snapped.

He caught up to her on the second floor, spinning her around to face him. "What is your problem?"

"Mine? My problem? You. That's right, you are my problem."

"How so?" He stepped closer to her.

She held her ground, refusing to give an inch. Even though she wanted to back up. Or was that jump into his embrace and see where it took them?

"You wouldn't even know anything about that damn pendant if not for me. Not only that, but also my grandmother's bag. I don't know these people and yet you want to *keep* me here while you go off with Mr Never Smiles." She rubbed her arm. "I wouldn't get in the way."

He cupped her shoulders then moved to her cheeks. "Listen to me, Taylor, and listen well. We're expecting to walk into a trap. I will not put you in danger. It's safest for you to remain here."

"What am I supposed to do while you're gone?"

"Whatever you want. Ride horses. Sleep. We both know it's been a while for you to have solid and uninterrupted sleep. Read. Help Billy and Edmond out with the pendant and what it means."

She brightened a bit. "I can do that still?"

"Yes. I'll tell them to expect you to be there helping them. I just need to know you're safe, Taylor. I'd much rather have you with me than Tiarnán. He's not nearly as soft as you are to curl up next to in bed. Plus he snores."

She chuckled while he grinned.

He pressed a cell phone into her hand. "Keep this with you so I can call and get in contact with you."

After a toe-curling kiss, she stood there on the stairs and watched him jog down to meet Tiarnán on the ground floor. Cale waved at her briefly before the men went outside.

Chapter Seven

The building was dark — a bonus to getting in unseen. Shoving his hands into his pockets, Cale walked up to the door.

"Ready, brother?"

"I'm waiting at the back looking at what used to be her balcony," Tiarnán spoke blandly.

"Used to be?"

"Part of the railing is missing and it looks like it wouldn't take much to knock it all the way down."

"Will you be okay?" If he thought about it, he would have realized how foolish his question was — Tiarnán was a warrior unlike any other they had. Yes, Dracen was a close second, but she still held back part of herself so he wasn't always sure who between the two of them was better.

"Of course. Let me know when you're at the door to her apartment. And no, I don't see anything lurking about out here. But still expect a trap."

He was. They honestly hadn't expected to see any demons — that would ruin their surprise. And it was always much better to let the creatures assume they had the upper hand, for they were quicker to make mistakes then.

As he walked up the flights of stairs to her floor, he didn't run into anyone. That was alarming in itself. Surely someone had to be going up or down. But nothing. Empty. Quiet. When he'd first gone to her place, they'd passed a couple of people on the stairs and in the halls. Now there was nothing.

Suspicious.

"I'm there." He felt his tattoo move as his power sped along his veins.

"I will be waiting, and there if and when they attack."

He allowed his senses to flare out—his heightened hearing and sense of smell. Just barely could he make out the lingering traces of human and demon. Nothing fresh, though. So if something was in there, he hadn't a clue what it would be.

Moving with caution, he opened the door and slipped inside silently. *"I'm in."*

"Anything?"

"Not yet. Nothing smells new. All I get is a hint of garlic."

"Garlic?"

"Just telling you what I smell, man."

"Get the bag and let's get out of here."

He moved through the room, stepping cautiously, trying to recall where she'd left the bag when the attack had come. Suddenly it was as if the walls came to life—demons peeled off them and swarmed him.

Even before he had a chance to call out, he heard the loud roar that accompanied Tiarnán. Silver *shuriken* slung through the darkness and pinned creatures to the wall. Then his fellow Chosen was at his side, weapons drawn as he battled against the swarm.

Cale threw his knives until he was out. Then he went to stars as well. It didn't make sense how many of them there were.

"*Eyes!*" Tiarnán cried in his head.

Immediately he ducked and covered his eyes. It didn't matter, the light piercing the room could still be seen. Demons screamed in agony before dying. He opened his eyes and got back into the battle. He went to his sword and continued slicing and dicing.

After chopping off the head of one, he turned in time to see a demon flying directly at him. It would have landed on the back of his head, but given he'd just spun around, it was coming for his face.

The mist rolled around him and the creature that had claimed him, making him a Guardian, snatched the approaching demon from the air and destroyed it with a single crunch of his jaws. *That was new.* His sign hadn't ever protected him like that before.

Although they were severely outnumbered, it didn't take them long before all the creatures lay dead. He stood amongst the rank and sulfur-smelling bodies and watched as Tiarnán gathered the weapons he'd thrown. Once his had been picked up, the men alternated positions and Cale grabbed his.

"Bag."

Tiarnán didn't speak all that much and Cale knew he was ready to get on his way. So he did a quick search of the apartment and found her bag. Gaudy, with its purple leopard print and gold lamé stitching. He grabbed the shoulder strap and frowned when a few more rainbow sparks exploded up.

"What was that?"

He shrugged. "I have no clue. Something left over from her touch, maybe? It was never far from her, she always touched it."

"Hmm."

Cale let it go — Tiarnán wouldn't be giving more than that. The sparks died down and he swung the bag over his shoulder before walking toward the door. Tiarnán fell into step beside him.

"Something on your mind?" he asked as they made their way down to the first floor.

"That seemed too easy."

"What are you thinking?"

"Something in the bag to track her location."

"We'll check it before we get home." He had no intention of bringing danger to Taylor.

They pushed into the night and drew up short. A group of four men stood there, discussing something amongst themselves. All of them lifted their heads when Cale and Tiarnán approached.

"Oh, hold that door please," the one in middle spoke.

Tiarnán was very deliberate in shutting it behind him.

"Sorry, you have to be let in by the person you're here to see." Cale adjusted the strap.

"You have my cousin's bag. We're here to see Taylor, do you know her?"

"Your cousin?" He tensed.

"What's wrong?"

"If these are truly her cousins, then they are after her to kill her."

"Remain calm."

"They want to kill my mate. Calm is a word that is no longer in my vocabulary."

"We have the advantage that they don't know who we are."

"Yes, Taylor Kenyon. We've been trying to reach her."

"She's not here. I'm her boyfriend."

Behind him, Tiarnán readjusted his stance and Cale fought a smile — he knew exactly how intimidating the man could be. Their eyes widened and it took a moment before they caught control of themselves.

"Boyfriend?"

"Cale Mattox. Who are you?"

"Jeremy Kenyon."

Cale stepped forward and offered his hand. The man sneered at him but took the outstretched hand. His shake was limp and damp. Cale hid his displeasure and released it quickly. There was no introduction of the others, nor of Tiarnán.

"Where's my cousin?"

"At my cabin. I just came back for her bag, since she forgot it." He moved the shoulder it hung from. "Would you like me to deliver a message?"

"I need to speak to her face to face."

"Okay, well, I'll let her know you were here and she can call you and set it up." He flashed a grin and began to move by them.

"How about we just follow you there and I can talk to her then?"

"Sorry, don't think that's a good idea. Does she have your number?" He shrugged. "I'm sure she does. I'll let her know to call you."

They walked around a corner and moved to the vehicle he'd rented. Unlocking the door, he then tossed her bag in and paused. As expected, the four had followed them.

Tiarnán got in his seat and Cale got in as well. "What do you think?" he asked.

"They want to hurt her. Shall we eliminate them?"

"You're getting more and more bloodthirsty, Tiarnán." He shook his head and pressed the start button for the engine. "Something going on with you?"

"Nope. Just asking a question."

That was one of the things he loved about his brother. The man might not be overly friendly to others, but he had Cale's back no matter what was about to go down. And he could fight.

They all had the same training, but the eldest man in their group of six had skills that were incredible. Hell, in the apartment Cale knew he could have just stood there and not worried—Tiarnán could have taken them all. Alone.

He fit his namesake—the tiger. He was a loner and a fierce protector of what he considered his. Luckily for the people who stayed at Tennesol Winery, Tiarnán considered all of them his.

Cale drove away and sure enough, as he'd expected, another vehicle pulled out behind him. "Company."

Tiarnán didn't even bother to turn around. "You can't bring them to her."

"Feeling protective?"

"We don't need more trouble at the vineyard."

"I'm not stupid, and we're not bringing them to her. We're going to bring her to them so they can talk. I'd really like to get some answers as to why they feel they can hunt her like a dog and want to kill her."

"So why am I bringing her when I can just extract the information from them?"

"You scare her and she's equating you to Wolverine."

Tiarnán glanced at him. "Wolverine?"

"Yes. I don't want her scared of you, so I want you to bring her here. Be nice to her." He pulled into the airport and dropped Tiarnán off. "Make it swift."

"I can handle this." There was no farewell, the man just strode off, his cowboy boots flashing with each of his long strides.

Cale shifted into gear and left the airport. Putting his hands free device in his ear, he used his phone to dial the woman he sought to talk to.

"Hello?" Her voice soothed the tension that had been building since the moment he left her.

"Taylor," he said.

"Did you find my bag, Cale?"

"Do you miss me?"

"Bag?"

"Lonely?" He grinned at the huff she sent across the line. "Come on, tell me."

"Yes, I miss you, but I'm having fun. Are you coming home?"

Home. Where she was. The idea was one he liked, immensely.

"Not yet. Tiarnán is going to come get you and bring you back here."

"Why?" Suspicion lanced her tone.

"I ran into your cousins, they were outside your apartment building."

"Jeremy?"

"Yes. They want to talk to you, so we'll do it. Just not at the vineyard. Be nice to Tiarnán when he arrives, babe."

"Me? Be nice to him? He's the one who looks like he wants to slit my throat."

He heard knocking behind her.

"I have to go." She hung up and he pressed the button.

"She's expecting you, Tiarnán."

"Don't sound so worried."

"How can I not?"

"We will be fine. Go rent a cabin somewhere and let me know where you are. We'll be there tomorrow."

* * * *

Taylor worried her lower lip as she sat on the top step leading to the house. She'd not slept much and was now waiting for Tiarnán to show and get her. A pickup rumbled up the drive and parked at the foot of the steps. Swallowing her fear, she pushed to her feet and walked down to the bottom.

Tiarnán met her at the door and held it for her. She had to stretch up to make it in his truck, but he didn't say a word. Once she'd settled on the seat, he closed the door behind her and she fastened her belt. Around the hood, he strode, the white of his shirt swathed broad shoulders and she shook her head. *Lord, he's built.* He moved like a predator and one she didn't want to be on the wrong side of.

The interior shrank when he climbed in. The slam of his door had her jerking slightly.

"I won't hurt you," he said.

"I know," she replied. She dampened her lips and tried not to curl up into a little ball.

He looked at her through strands of dark hair, which fell over his hazel eyes. She waited for him to say something else, but he didn't. Instead, he shifted gears and got them heading back down the driveway. She hugged the door and tried desperately to calm her racing heart and stop sweating like she was. It wasn't happening—she had this innate fear of him and she couldn't explain it.

Tiarnán drove into the airport long term parking and put them in a spot after grabbing the ticket. He was at her door by the time she managed to unbuckle her belt. She wiped off her damp palm and took his outstretched hand. He was strength personified.

"Ready?"

She shook her head. "Yes."

"We won't let them hurt you."

"Why do you care?" she asked as they walked toward the front door of the airport.

"Because you are important to Cale."

She grabbed his arm and after a brief — maybe longer than that — moment of admiration for the cut muscles beneath her hand, she said, "Wait. You're doing this for Cale?"

"Yes. He asked me to come get you."

"You said we won't let them hurt you. How many are there?"

"When I left him, there were four following him."

She clutched at her chest. "Four? Is he okay?"

"Four are no issue for him. He will be fine."

"Are you sure?"

"Yes." He held her gaze and she shifted beneath his intense hazel stare. "He will be fine."

She released her grip on him and nodded. They began walking again. "Do you not like me?"

"I don't know you well enough to like you or not."

"Do you have a problem with me because of my skin color?"

It was his turn to stop and he did, staring down at her with a confused expression. "You have seen my family, right?"

"Some of them, yes."

He glanced around the airport then focused back on her. "You and I will never have a problem unless you hurt Cale. I will keep you safe so long as there is breath in my body. You are a sister now. Does that clear it up?"

She smiled, reached up on her tiptoes and kissed his cheek. "Do I get to call you big brother?"

When he smiled, the man was positively, devastatingly handsome. "You, precious, can call me whatever you want."

She slipped her arm through his and rested her head along his upper arm. "I'll remember that."

Grateful to have that uncertainty taken care of, she felt so much better, and a bit silly for having even had the fear. Tiarnán got their tickets and, side by side, they passed through security. She shook her head — they were in first class — but she wasn't about to argue with him on it.

"Sleep," he said as they sat.

"Are you sure?"

"You look like you didn't sleep much. Rest now."

She used him as her pillow and smiled softly when a blanket settled over her. "You're not as scary as you come across, Tiarnán."

* * * *

He woke her before they landed. On the ground, since they had no luggage, it didn't take them long to head through baggage claim and out to the front. She couldn't explain the joy when she saw Cale waiting for her beside a car.

"I missed you," he said, gathering her close for a tight hug. Her legs trembled when he brushed their lips together. "He didn't bother you too much with his moodiness, did he?"

"Be nice to my big brother," she said, slipping her arms around Cale's waist and winking at Tiarnán.

"Big brother?"

"Yes, I can call him that."

"Can you now?" he rumbled.

She had a feeling the men were talking amongst themselves in their heads. Closing her eyes, she just waited for them to finish. Cale led her to the car and helped her into the backseat. The two men slipped in the front and they were on their way.

"Jeremy and his boys were lurking around the cabin yesterday evening."

Cold poured in her veins and she wrapped her arms around herself as she wished for Cale's warmth, or at least a blanket.

"Are you sure you two can handle them?"

Cale met her gaze in the rear view mirror. "After fighting demons, babe, humans are a lot less difficult to go against. Besides, if you keep questioning our...my...ability to protect you, you're going to give me a complex."

His comment made her smile. "Sorry."

He blew her a kiss then pressed on the accelerator and shot off down the road.

She dozed again and woke when they went over a bump. She sat up with a yawn and glanced out of the window. They passed some cabins as they moved along the dirt road. All of it surrounded a lake. When he pulled up to a cabin, she felt a surge of energy pour through her.

Taylor climbed out and stretched. Cale joined her and popped the trunk. They each took some of the grocery bags and entered the small cabin. First thing she noticed was there were only two bedrooms. Shaking that off, she placed the items down and let Cale put them away.

Tiarnán vanished and she began twitching and moving things around, unsure of what she should do. "They'll be here soon," Cale informed her.

"How do you know?"

"Because they show up about ten minutes after the car is parked."

"Where's Tiarnán?"

"Near." He stood in front of her and kissed her. She moaned into his mouth as her arms closed about his neck.

"How near?" she murmured against his lips.

The chuckle he emitted made her smile. "Near. Don't worry, babe. Tonight it's all about you and me."

Heat spiraled out from within her and she bit the inside of her lip. "Perfect."

The knock on the door had her tensing. Cale kissed her once more then went to open it.

Her breathing hitched when it swung open to put her face to face with Jeremy. Cale didn't say a word, just gestured in her direction. When her cousin's beady eyes landed on her, she gulped and stood straighter.

Bastard. I'm not scared of you. Okay, so I am, but I'm not running from you.

"Taylor! I've been looking everywhere for you."

I just bet you have. "I've been here and there. Needed some time after Grandma's passing."

"Right. Can we go somewhere and talk?"

"No. We were about to start on dinner, so you can say whatever it is you need to before me and Cale."

"Yes, Cale. Your boyfriend."

He called himself my boyfriend. "What about him?"

"I didn't know you were dating anyone. When did this start?"

She narrowed her gaze. "None of your business. What did you need to see me about? We have plans for the evening."

The men behind him moved and she glanced up to see Tiarnán entering, his broad shoulders forcing the others out of his way.

Jeremy frowned and glanced between all three of them. "Wait, is he one of your boyfriends as well?"

Tiarnán stiffened before peering at her with one eyebrow raised a bit. *Oh yeah, this is going to be fun.* She plastered a smile on her face. "Of course. We're all one happy couple."

Cale pinched her on the ass, but she couldn't bring herself to stop. Not yet.

"I found out a while ago I needed two men to make me happy, sexually."

Color drained from his face. She blinked and leaned into Cale. "Did I shock you? I'm sorry. I thought we were old enough to speak frankly."

"What…what about Dale?" He gestured behind him.

She looked at the boy she used to date. Boy, not man. She waved at him. "What about him? He wasn't good enough in bed and wasn't all that fun. These two are…wow."

Jeremy cleared his throat, tried unsuccessfully to wipe the shock from his face and said, "I need the charm from Grandma."

"Sorry. She gave it to me, I'm not giving it over to you." She licked her lips, fortified by the knowledge the two men with her would keep her safe. At least for now. "I know you're trying to kill me, but know this. I don't have it on me so if you do, you'll still never get your greedy hands on it."

"Kill you? You're family."

"Family you've never wanted. We really don't have anything to say to one another, so why don't you leave?"

He shook his head. "I'd really hoped it wouldn't come to this." Jeremy drew his piece and the others who'd fanned out before the door did as well.

Five guns pointed at them. Fear? Yep, she had it in spades.

Cale moved his body in front of her. "You want to put them away."

"No. I want that fucking pendant."

"One last chance." Cale's tone was hard and unyielding.

"There's five of us and three of you."

Cale shook his head. "Actually there's two of you and three of us."

"Need to learn to count, dude."

Cale shrugged and she counted. *Shit. He's right. What happened to the others?* "Where'd they go?" she asked.

"Tiarnán." Cale's explanation was relaxed.

"And he left two for you why?"

"He wanted me to feel like I was protecting you."

Jeremy glanced over his shoulder and saw he was alone with Dale. There was no sign of the other men he'd arrived with. "What the fuck, man?"

Cale moved with a blur of explosive motion. Taylor saw it happen but wasn't sure she believed it. In less time than it took her to blink, he'd disarmed and knocked Dale unconscious. Jeremy was between Cale and the wall, feet off the ground as Cale shoved his face up to his.

She wasn't sure what to do. Should she stop him? Would he kill Jeremy?

Chapter Eight

Cale snarled at the man he held against the wall. He wanted to reach in through Jeremy's mouth and rip out his spine. The man's eyes were wide with fear and panic.

"Let me make one thing clear," he rumbled. "You look at Taylor sideways again and think that in some way you can get that pendant she received from her grandmother, not to mention kill her, I will introduce to you a world of pain you can't even begin to imagine."

"You can't do this," Jeremy sputtered.

He sneered. "I'm doing it. You're alone now. The *crew* you traveled with isn't here to back you up. Do you really think you can take me? You hide behind the threat of your gun, now you don't even have that anymore."

"She's my family and I don't know what lies she's told you, but I don't want to kill her. We've been searching for her to bring her home."

Cale's power moved within him and he struggled to control it. Never before had the urge to kill been so strong within him. "No woman stays in a place where there are huge bugs on the floor for no reason when she has a home to go to unless death awaits her there. Your lies reek and I despise people who can't own up to what they've done."

Jeremy's expression grew defiant. "Fine. We wanted to kill the bitch. She shouldn't have been part of the family anyway. She was only around because grandmother refused to let one of her father's offspring, no matter how illegitimate, not be in the family. She always said we had to own up to our mistakes. And that's what she is, a mistake."

Cale tightened his hand around the neck he held. Jeremy gasped but still maintained his smug arrogance.

"She wasn't ever wanted. Not by any of us."

"So why try to kill her? Why not just let her go?"

"That pendant is worth millions. We looked it up one day before she died and had plans to sell it. When the old bitch died she gave it to *her*."

"Which is where it will stay. Listen to me and listen well. You even sneeze in her direction again and I'll find you. When I do, you'll wish you were dead because I'm really good at making your desire for death last a long time."

"You can't threaten me."

"I just did. And if she wasn't here watching us right now, I'd kill you. Just because I don't think you're anything more than a waste of oxygen and space in the universe. You and your stupid friends." He took another deep breath to try to calm down. "Let me repeat this. Taylor is mine, got it? *Mine.* And I will die to protect her, and go through whomever or whatever is sent after her to keep her safe. You don't know what you're messing with because if you think by killing me, you'll get to her, you're wrong. She's well protected and will always be." He leaned closer. "Forget her, forget the pendant. Live longer."

"You and I will meet again."

Cale's smile was feral. "I do hope so. I can't wait to strip the flesh from your bones. This was a warning meeting. I see you again, I will learn what your blood looks like."

"You're sick, man."

"I'm a man who will do anything to protect his woman." Sparks began to flash along his skin.

"What...what is that?"

"My power."

"Power?" Jeremy's word more resembled a gasp than anything.

"Yes." He stared down his nose at Jeremy. "Do us both a favor and never show your face around us again."

"What about my friends?"

"Hope they're still alive, I don't know. Tiarnán is the warrior and looks at Taylor as his. He's very protective of her as well."

"We'll go, let me down and we'll go."

Cale squeezed tighter then dropped him. Jeremy hit the ground with a whimper and rubbed at the mark on his neck before scrambling to his feet and bolting out of the door. Cale turned once he'd vanished to spy the woman standing behind him. Taylor watched him with wide eyes and her hands were knotted before her.

He beckoned to her. "Come here."

She followed his directive and moved into his embrace. Cale wrapped his arms around her and buried his nose into her hair.

"He'll not bother you again."

"I thought you were going to kill him."

"I wanted to," he admitted.

She didn't move away. "I'm glad you didn't."

"Why?"

"He's an asshole and a jerk, but I don't want you to have his death on your conscious."

"Make no mistake, Taylor Kenyon. I would kill for you. And I'd die for you."

She pulled back, staring intently at his expression. "Why?"

"Why?"

She nodded.

"Because you are my mate."

"But that could have been anyone."

He shook his head. "No."

"Yes. You didn't know who would set off that spark thingy. It could have been anyone. I'm not special and while I thank you for standing up to Jeremy for me, I don't need more than that."

"You aren't seeing what I do." He had to get her to understand.

"So explain it to me."

He led her to the couch and sat beside her. Propping an arm along the back, he held her hand with his other.

"You see this as you could have been anyone. That any person could be sitting here with me that causes the rainbow display of sparks."

"Exactly."

He brushed back a few strands of the diagonal fringe from her forehead and allowed his touch to linger along her smooth skin before returning his hand to the couch.

"Allow me to enlighten you, Taylor. I see this, *us*, as something beyond our comprehension. I'm sitting across from a woman who was handpicked for me. There could be no other because not any other person could give me what you can. The Guardians have been given a task that's dangerous. We didn't have a choice, but we're given…extra to help us deal with it. The ones who are our mates don't have extras like we have, and in my estimation, they have to be extremely special to put up with us and what we're going to go through." He squeezed her hand. "You are, in my estimation, the stronger of the two of us. And you were put here for me. No one else has the strength to do what you will and give to me that which I need."

She tipped her head to the side and he gave a small smile.

"You, Taylor, out of the millions of people in the world, were picked for me. That doesn't make you 'just anyone', it makes you so special and unique."

"What are we going to go through?"

He sighed. "I don't know. If I knew, I'd let you know. But I haven't a clue and Lian isn't exactly being forthcoming with whatever it is on the horizon for us." He spied the flash of fear and uncertainty in her eyes and squeezed her hand. "I will protect you."

"What about you? Who's going to protect you?"

He jerked his head toward the door. "Well, I do have Wolverine at my back."

While shaky, she at least produced a smile. "I don't want anything to happen to either of you." Turning her head, she asked, "Where is he?"

"Tiarnán took them somewhere else."

"So we're alone?"

He stared at her and nodded. "Completely and utterly."

Heat flared in her eyes as her pupils dilated. "Good to know."

"*We need to talk.*"

"Oh, the misty thing is happening. Someone contacting you?"

He grunted. "Billy." Damn the man for interrupting him now.

Taylor allowed her touch to skim over his cock before she got to her feet. "Handle what you need to. I'll fix some food. Will Tiarnán be back for the meal?"

He turned his head and watched her walk, the sway of her hips making him think of things that had nothing to do with talking to Billy at all. Nor did it deal with thinking about Tiarnán. "Nope."

"Okay."

"*What is it, Billy?*"

"*Edmond figured out the other symbols, both on the chain and pendant.*"

"*And this couldn't wait until we got back?*"

"*No. Listen. The symbol on the pendant we didn't know before is* storm. *However, when we ran the ones from the chain through the system we got hit.*"

"*A hit?*"

"*No. Hits as in someone was looking specifically for those words. Members of The New Order. So they're on even higher alert now. There've been some odd sightings going on over in Scotland, which Lian has said to be the work of Uma. I'm going over there to see what I can find. Maybe I will hit paydirt and find another artifact.*"

"*Be careful.*"

"*You know me, I always am. But I am also a thief, so I can steal it if that's what it comes down to. He just thinks that if Uma or some of the ones with her are there, they must have a lead.*"

"*How does that work though, if there's no sign of anything between this person and their mate?*"

"*They may just know what the artifact should look like and be after it. If it's in a museum or buried somewhere,*" perhaps I can get to it and bring it back to the vineyard for safe keeping."

"When do you leave?"

"Tomorrow I'm heading out. I won't see you until I get back. So stay safe."

"You too."

Their connection broke off and Cale sat there for a moment, running over what he'd just learnt.

"Everything okay?"

Pivoting around so he could see Taylor, he was touched by the concern in her expression. "I hope so."

Taylor watched him as the mist that surrounded him when he talked in his mind to his brethren settled back into his skin. She could stare at him all day without it being a problem. *It'd be perfectly okay by me to do so.*

Right now, it seemed something was wrong. "You hope so? What's going on?"

In for a penny, in for a pound. She was in this and might as well learn as much as she could.

"Billy is going to Scotland."

"How wonderful." She pursed her lips, canting her head to the side. "Isn't it?"

"I'm not so sure. There've been reports of some destruction going on over there. Lian said it sounds like one of the creatures we're going to have to fight against. So he, Billy, is heading there to see if they've discovered an artifact."

Destruction? What the hell am I missing by not watching the news? "What happens if they have? He can't take it from them, can he?" *I'm talking about 'they' and 'them' as if I'm part of this whole insane fiasco.*

"Before he came to the vineyard, Billy was a thief. And a damn good one. His skills haven't diminished.

If anything, they've gotten better. His sign is the monkey and it's given him an added bonus of agility and sneakiness. So he can take it from them if they have it."

"You're concerned for what reason, then?"

"We're not so close if he needs us."

"Is his mate there?"

"No clue. He's just going to check out the supposed destruction which is going on."

"I'm sure he'll be fine." She began to mix a salad. Her cooking skills weren't all that good, but she could make a meal.

"I hope so too." Cale moved to help her in the kitchen.

"So, you're the healer and carry the sign of the dog. Billy is the monkey and is a thief, what are the others?"

"Tiarnán is the tiger. He's our best warrior and he can camouflage to just about anything. Roz carries the sign of the horse. Swiftness is her attribute. Aminta has the ram sign. I say it gives her stubbornness. And Dracen is the dragon. We're not sure what it gives her. She's got a bit of us all in her and more."

"She's quiet."

"And our second best warrior."

She chopped some tomatoes. "Better than you?"

His chuckle came swiftly. "Oh definitely. She can kick my ass without really trying. Fights with her and Tiarnán take on a life of their own. One day she'll beat him but right now, he ends up on top."

"Are they together?"

"Together? As in mates?"

"Yes. They're very close."

"Siblings only. They've been here, well at the vineyard, the longest of all who are there now."

She watched him put the steaks in the pan to sear them. "And you weren't with anyone there?"

"That's family there, darling. That's all." He moved in close and brushed his lips along the nape of her neck, causing her to shiver. "Those women are my sisters and I have never, ever, nor will I ever want to share with them that which you and I have."

His words created a warm ball in her belly. There was no way around it—there was proof she was falling for this man, more and more each day. It didn't make sense, but she couldn't argue with the facts presented right before her.

"Are we going back to the mansion?"

"Yes. Need to get a bit more information and see what, if anything, is in the bag from your grandmother."

She nodded, hoping that didn't mean they had to destroy it. They finished preparing dinner, the talk swinging to something lighter. The mood lasted through the meal and the dessert that followed.

As she rinsed off the last dish, she glanced over her shoulder and watched Cale wipe off the table. Every motion he produced had her mind replaying what it had been like in bed with him back in Oregon.

"You can keep making those cute little noises, Taylor, but I promise you'll be in a bed on your back naked, if you do so."

Her hand trembled and she nearly dropped the plate she held. It took her a few attempts to swallow and ensure her legs wouldn't give out from under her. The flash of teeth she caught from him told her he knew what thoughts had crossed through her mind at his words.

"Promises, promises."

He'd lowered his head but at her two words, it snapped up and his dark blue eyes flared with a passion that nearly burned her from across the room. His desire and need were so intermixed, she couldn't tell one from the other.

She fumbled until the water shut off, but that was all the moving she did. She felt like prey. Dampening her lips, she attempted to slide to the right slightly, but his gaze narrowed on her when she did.

The rag fell from his hands to the tabletop and she bolted. No destination in mind, just running. She squealed when he scooped her up and tossed her over his shoulder. Gripping the back of his shirt, she avoided staring at his ass — sort of. She jumped when he smacked her on the butt, an act that sent tingles all through her, especially to her clit.

When she bounced on the mattress, she merely looked up at him, a saucy grin on her face. He leaned over her, blocking her in with strong arms and put his face close. "You're playing with fire, Taylor."

She dragged her tongue along her lower lip as she reached out to mess with the collar of his shirt. "Am I? How so?"

"I am barely holding on here," he said.

Wrapping her legs around the backs of his, she jerked him closer. "So let go."

They must have been the words he had been waiting for. Cale rumbled low in his chest and in a quick moment, her clothes were gone. So were his, for his hot naked body pressed her back into the mattress.

"Wow, that was impressive," she sighed.

"You ain't seen nothin' yet, babe."

"And there he goes with the promises again."

"Ones you can take to the bank."

He flipped her over, ignored her screech and began kissing his way up her body. Starting from the sole of her foot up to where her hair hung on her neck, he licked, laved and nipped her into a fervor. When he laid her on her back, she reached for him.

"No. You have to stay still."

She scrunched her fingers in the top covering of the bed—whatever it was, she hadn't taken the time to notice it. Hard to notice anything other than the man with her. He went back down to her feet and picked one up, placing the sole against his shoulder. Dragging his index finger up and down her calf, he merely stared at her.

"Stop torturing me," she begged.

"I've not even begun to torture you yet." His words were deep and dark.

Her belly clenched as she tried not to squirm beneath his touch and stare. "Please."

He kissed her big toe. "Nope."

Farther and farther up her body he moved. Her gaze locked on his large cock, which stood out from his pelvis. The pre-cum on the head had her wanting to taste him. Feel him slide in and out of her lips as she knelt between his legs. More moisture went to her pussy and she wriggled on the bed.

"Cale," she gasped.

"Not done yet," he muttered as he passed up over her sternum to her neck. The rasp of his stubble heightened her pleasure as he continued to keep her on the edge of her orgasm.

His hard length slipped against her slit and she moaned, widening her legs to welcome more of his weight. Rotating her hips, she moved up and down along him. He tensed above her before capturing her earlobe and sucking it in time with her own movements.

Releasing the blanket, she then gripped him. The feel of his flesh beneath her fingers brought her a sense of relief, for being able to touch him, but also skyrocketed her need. She dug her grip into him, hard, as she locked her legs around him.

Cale slipped a hand between them and readjusted his hard cock. She purred as it filled her, one inch at a time. He didn't rush and when he was fully seated inside her, she cracked her eyes open and stared at him. The misty look he had when he was talking to his brethren covered his entire body, yet at the same time, different. Warmer almost, if she could give it that description. Beneath her fingers, his muscles rippled and moved as he stroked in her.

"Cale," she whispered.

"Let me," his response fell.

Let him? Like she wanted anything else. In and out he thrust, not rushing, just leaving her with a long, deep burn for release. Rainbow sparks lit the mist around him and moved to encompass her as well. She closed her eyes again and lost herself in the touch of this man.

It was gentle. Slow. Drugging.

Taylor screamed as she came around his cock, the pleasure washing over her too intense to keep the sounds contained within her. Cale drove into her four more times before he spilled his load deep inside her. She whimpered as mini orgasms cropped up and shot through her entire body.

He nearly collapsed on her, turning at the last minute to ensure he didn't crush her. Still deep in her pussy, he wrapped his arms around her and repositioned them so she lay on top of him.

He didn't speak, just stared at her and brushed some more hair off her forehead. She ducked her head and placed it on his chest, listening to the fast beating of his heart. The sparks still danced along their skin.

"Do you see the rainbow of colors?" he asked, smoothing a hand up and down the bare skin of her back.

"I do. It's weird. Almost feels like they're massaging my skin. And yet, not. If that makes any sense."

"It does."

She groaned as he flexed his hips.

"More."

Taylor didn't argue. She wanted more as well, and if she were completely honest with herself, she didn't know how long they had with one another, not given how dire this upcoming battle sounded.

Sitting up, she placed her hands on his chest and rotated her hips. "Yes, more."

Chapter Nine

Cale struggled not to lose his temper as he squared off with Tiarnán in the practice room. *Danger Room.* Taylor's term for it came to him and again made him smile.

"Shit!" he cried, ducking a swipe from Tiarnán.

The man didn't let up, his *katana* barely paused before it was on another attack path.

"Pay attention."

He was, damn it all. "I am." His arms ached from the clash of metal. Tiarnán was one strong mother fucker.

"Pay attention to the battle, not thoughts of your woman."

It rankled—that the man could read him so well. He'd woken this morning with every intention of making his way to Taylor's room and spending time in there with her. No clothing and lots of exploration between the two of them. Nothing had gone his way. First Lian had wanted to see him, then he'd had some kids to oversee and now this...this ass-whipping he was being hand-delivered by Tiarnán.

He sneered. "Don't be jealous just because you don't have one and are stuck jacking off at night in your room to find any semblance of relief."

Cale didn't mean the words, they just slipped out. However, that one second flash on Tiarnán's face was like he'd just took a bullet to the chest. The emotion was there and gone so fast, it could have been imagined.

"You'll be doing the same if you don't concentrate, because your woman will be dead." Tiarnán moved with a flurry of speed and disarmed Cale, the blade of his *katana* resting against Cale's throat. "You spend too much time thinking about her and what you'd rather be doing. You need to focus."

"Let's go again."

Tiarnán shook his head, dark hair flying about his face as he stepped back, lowering the weapon and sheathing it with a singular, smooth move. "No. Your mind is not where it should be."

"You're the one who said I had to practice."

He strode to the door. "You do. And so do I, but it's not practice for me if you're not thinking about what you need to do. Therefore it is a waste of my time."

The door closed behind him and Cale stared at it, shaking his head in disbelief. It opened again, this time admitting Taylor. She walked up to him and placed a hand on his arm.

"I just saw Tiarnán leave, I thought you were practicing for a lot longer. Are you hurt?"

"No, I'm an ass, is what I am."

She withdrew her touch from him and he regretted it immediately. "I'm sorry, Taylor. What are you doing here?"

Her shoulders rose and fell. "I was going to see if I could watch you practice."

"Maybe tomorrow, babe. I haven't been concentrating today."

"Is that why he left?"

His smile was forced. "Yes. Tiarnán doesn't like to waste time. If we're not doing it at least one hundred percent, he will stop."

"Isn't some practice better than none?"

"Not if you're not fully committed to doing it. The enemy won't come at you half-assed, so why practice that way." He put an arm around her shoulders. "It's why he is the best warrior."

"Need you in the ops room."

"On my way, Dracen."

"Who called?" Taylor asked.

"What?"

"You did that misty-smoky thing again. Do you have to go?"

He nodded with understanding. "I do. It was Dracen. Come on."

Her smile warmed him. "No thanks. They didn't ask for me. You go. I'm going to explore."

He narrowed his eyes. "Are you sure?"

"Positive." She shooed at him with her hands. "Go. Do your non-mutant, X-Man things."

"Woman," he warned.

"What?" she sassed with a grin. "I said non-mutant." Taylor headed off down the hall with a wave over her shoulder.

Cale didn't move until she'd vanished from sight. Then and only then did he head off in the opposite direction. Stepping through the sliding doors into the room they had turned into their operations room, he immediately noticed all the women were there. Billy, still being in Scotland, he hadn't expected, but he had Tiarnán. The man wasn't present.

"Where's Tiarnán?"

"Practicing." Aminta gave him a knowing smile.

They all knew he practically lived to fight and at most times could be found with some sort of weapon in his hand, or with their weapons maker, honing one thing or another.

He glanced around the room again. "With Lian?"

"Yes." Roz opened the top on her Coke and took a large drink.

Cale took his usual chair and rested his arms against the table. "So what's up?"

Dracen hit a key and a few photos popped up. He frowned when he recognized the faces there—Jeremy Kenyon and his family. A low growl slipped from his lips.

"I take it then you know them?" Dracen asked.

"Remember the 'family' I told you was trying to kill Taylor? That's him. Tiarnán and I just had a run in with them, that's why I had him bring her to where I was." He gestured with his chin. "What's the reason we have pics of them?"

"They're New Order."

"New Order?"

"We just got confirmation today." Aminta slid a file across the smooth top toward him.

Staring briefly at the small Asian woman—Amerasian, technically—who was his sister and a fellow Guardian, he waited for her to continue. Her straight black hair fell around her sculpted face.

"We intercepted a few calls from them back to someone named Blake."

He shook his head, the name unfamiliar to him. "That's it, Blake? Nothing more to go on?"

"We hadn't heard of him either, so he's new to The Order or just new on the scene."

"Do we have a location on him?"

"Still working on that part. We thought maybe you could ask Taylor for a bit more information on these guys. Find out what they're into, where they hang out, things like that." Roz fiddled with her bottle.

"Are we worrying about The New Order now?"

Dracen clicked off the screen and sat. "We're always worried about them, Cale. We're just thinking that if we can find our way to someone who's at the top, or near the top, maybe, just maybe we can have a bit more insight on what those bastards are planning and if they have a timeline they're working with. Look, we all know that Lian isn't going to tell us anything more than he can." She sighed. "I love the man to death, but let's face it, he's bound by older rules of what he can and can't say. Even if he could say, most of what he imparts is in riddle."

Cale drummed his fingers on the table. "Why isn't Tiarnán here for this?"

"We've already talked to him about it." Dracen leaned back and put her booted feet up on the table.

"So this decision has already been made?"

"Absolutely not. If you don't feel talking to Taylor about this, we can go another route." Roz finished off her Coke and also leaned back.

"So you wouldn't force this?"

"Why would we? We're just trying to figure out a way to get ahead. We all know those of The New Order and those commanding them will break rules. Lian—our link to all this, won't, he has too much honor for that. We have to find our own ways. She was a thought," Roz said.

There were some days he forgot Roz was the youngest woman there. Youngest of the six, in fact. She had a sharp mind and had excelled at school once she'd arrived here. In fact, at twenty, she was one of the youngest attorneys around. No one underestimated her though, not anymore.

"I'll talk to her. Can't promise anything."

"A chance is all we're looking for," Dracen stated. "We need some kind of edge or we're going to be slaughtered before we have a chance to make it to this 'huge battle' we have been training for."

The anger and concern in her voice worried him. Dracen didn't show emotion and she didn't get rattled. At least not until he'd found his artifact—like his was the first and had set off some kind of chain reaction throughout the world. He glanced to his left, where they'd put the gold pendant and chain. The pendant was even more gold now and the symbols had turned black, as if they'd been painted on. Or burned. He wasn't sure, but it had changed dramatically since the first time he'd seen it. Five empty boxes sat near it for the other pieces they desperately needed to find in order to fulfill the prophesy. More of what concerned not only him, but the others as well.

* * * *

Taylor smiled to herself and readjusted on the large chaise as she read further into the book on art history. She loved the subject, and this humongous library Lian had contained so many books on that very thing.

She reached for her iced tea sitting on a coaster beside her, only to come up empty. She frowned and tipped the book toward her chest and looked. Cale stood there, taller than life, staring down at her. He held her tea.

"You scared me," she said lightly. "Done with your meeting?"

"I am." He handed over the glass when she beckoned with her fingers. "I see you've made yourself at home."

"I did. Went to the kitchen and made some tea, properly I might add. Drank two glasses there before filling one and tracking down this room. I've been in here reading since."

"Proper tea?"

"Sweet."

"So just add sugar to the stuff we have."

Her face contorted and she shook her head violently. "That is *not* proper." One hand rose and she took several deep breaths. "Anyway. That's neither here nor there. I have the right kind of tea. How was your thing?"

His expression sobered. When he lowered himself to the chaise by her feet, she knew it couldn't be good news. One more sip then she put her glass down on the coaster.

"We need your help."

"Okay. What with?"

"We need some information you can give, any and all you can depart with."

She blinked, waiting for more detail. "Okay," she drew out. "Information on what?"

"Jeremy Kenyon and the guys who were with him."

Warnings snaked up her spine instantly and she struggled not to give away her fear. "What do you need to know about them?"

He touched her ankle and began rubbing it. "Anything. Everything. Places they hung out. What they liked doing. All of that."

"Can I ask why?"

"We discovered they're linked to The New Order."

Momentarily speechless, she just sat there, fingers flexing around the edges of the art history book. "My cousins?"

He nodded. "It explains why they thought the pendant would be worth so much. Whoever hired them to get it over exaggerated its monetary worth."

"So...wait...are you saying...?" She gulped and breathed deep a few times. "Are you saying they killed my grandmother to get this thing from her? And when the will gave it to me, they came after me?"

He shook his head. "I don't know, babe. We can find out if you want. All I know for certain is they are working with men from The New Order and we really need to find out for who, and get as high up the ladder we can.

Good Lord, she was nauseated. "Sure. I'll give you what I can. When? Now?"

"As soon as you're up to it."

She closed the book and swung her feet to the floor. "Don't know if I will ever be, not knowing they may have purposefully killed her. Let's get it over with."

Taylor replaced the book on the shelf and turned to find Cale there holding her tea. He placed a light kiss along her lips and she gave him a half-smile before taking the tea then heading for the door.

"Where are we doing this?"

"The room with all the computers."

As they walked along the spotless halls, she did her best to psyche herself up. The mixed emotions that warred within her didn't make sense. She owed Jeremy no loyalty and yet she felt almost like she was betraying him. The heavy doors slid open before her and they walked in together. Five faces stared back at her.

Four she recognized and one she didn't. The women gave her a brief smile while Tiarnán nodded sharply. She took a chair beside the one she knew Cale usually sat in.

"Thanks for helping us out, Taylor," Roz spoke from across the table. "I believe you know everyone here."

"No," she glanced down to the one she didn't recognize. "I don't know him."

"Sorry," Cale said beside her. "Edmond Stanton, this is Taylor Kenyon. Taylor, Edmond. Our resident computer genius."

He smiled at her, his white teeth brilliant against his black skin. "My pleasure, Taylor."

Instantly he set her at ease and she found herself returning his grin. "Good to meet you, Edmond."

Cale placed his arm along the back of her chair. Taylor wasn't sure whether it was just because, or if he somehow felt threatened by Edmond. She leaned forward, clasped her hands and focused on the man with his fingers hovering over the keyboard.

"Ready when you are, Taylor," Edmond said.

"You have all their names?" When he nodded, she canted her head to the side. "Jeremy liked to hang out at pool bars. He and those with him enjoyed trying to hustle games from newcomers to the bars or clubs. I know one of his favorite places was one called The Rack. According to him, it had it all."

"Where was this place?"

"Near Beaufort, which is on Port Royal Island."

"Where did you live?" Cale asked her softly.

"Charleston."

She struggled not to think about how growing up had been. They were here to do something specific and surely she could control her own memories long enough to help them accomplish it. Swallowing some more tea, she waited for the next question.

That was how it went for the next few hours. She gave them all she could on Jeremy and the men in the pictures beside him. Emotionally drained at the end of it, she walked out at their thanks and headed for her room.

When she got there, she discovered a tall glass of tea sitting out beside the longue on the balcony. She moved slowly to it and saw the lemon and mint floating in it. Cautiously, she sipped some then moaned in pleasure as the sweet beverage ran down her throat. Sitting on the lounger, she replaced the glass and stared through the railings.

Grass waved in the warm breeze, the sun shined down and played tag with the few fluffy clouds in the sky. She could hear the horses and the children but didn't move to see if she could actually lay eyes upon them.

Even more emotionally tired than before, she allowed her eyes to drift closed. When she opened them again, a blanket covered her and the sun was low in the sky. To her left, a figure lurked in the corner of the balcony. Cale. She would know his body anywhere.

"Feeling better?" he asked, pushing away and moving toward her.

"How long have you been there?"

"About an hour."

"Isn't that stalking?" she teased. "You there, watching me while I'm sleeping?"

"Maybe." Cale crouched beside her. "Are you feeling better?"

No she wasn't—she still felt extremely betrayed. Not only did her cousins want to kill her, but they had possibly joined with this New Order and had her grandmother killed. She hadn't been well loved in that house, but her grandmother had been all she had. She'd fed her and had put a roof over her. Not only that, but she'd learned how to act in many situations, even if, again, the love wasn't there.

"I suppose so."

"Talk to me."

"Just frustrated by all of this. I mean, I know I wasn't supposed to be part of the family and only was because Grandmother refused to let my father get away with his indiscretion and ignore me. I was raised as a woman with wealth and had to fit in with that life. She only gave me the bag a few weeks before she passed. Told me that she was sorry she didn't give me more, that everyone should do something outrageous, then cleared her throat and walked out of the room."

Damn it! She hated the tears that threatened every time she relived this.

Chapter Ten

She wrapped her arms around herself and Cale wanted to replace them with his own embrace. He hated she had those emotions swarming in her. The afternoon had been tough on her, he knew that—they all knew that—yet she'd never once complained. There were times she'd even tried to insert some humor, even though he knew it had cost her a great effort to pull it off.

Deciding he'd had enough, Cale slid his body onto the chaise, half lifting her to settle upon his lap. She didn't fight him, in fact it was quite the opposite. Taylor tucked her head below his chin and burrowed in closer. Lacing his fingers, he readjusted so she sat between his legs and he had his arms around her, keeping her close and sharing body heat in the cool evening with the breeze going around them. She reached out and drew the blanket over them as well.

Nose buried in her hair, he too, dozed off. The moon was rising when he woke. Taylor still slept in his embrace and he barely moved, for he had no wish to wake her.

"We are making headway with the information she gave us, Cale."

"I'll let her know when she wakes up, Aminta, thank you."

"We figured she was sleeping or something like that when you missed coming down for dinner."

"We fell asleep on her chaise."

"Is that what we're calling it now? Interesting. I thought it had a different name. And I have heard you look hot in nothing but a pink towel."

He rolled his eyes at her comments. She had a great sense of humor, remarkable really when she was a one hell of a pilot and used to flying into situations most wouldn't dream of dealing with. But Aminta hid a side—her humorous one—from all but those she considered family.

"Don't need that spreading around."

"Too late. Everyone knows. I think even Edmond is making you an avatar to have on the computer so you feel...um...loved."

"I am so kicking your ass when I see you next."

"You'll be too tired." She laughed. *"Which inevitably will give me the advantage."*

"G'nite, trouble."

"Oh, I'm not going to bed yet. I have work to do. But I will tell you good night."

She broke the connection and he smiled, all the while gathering Taylor close. He had one hell of a family. He allowed his eyes to drift shut again, the night air filled with familiar scents and one that played havoc on his libido and yet simultaneously soothed his soul.

* * * *

He woke with a jerk. Something was wrong. Taylor stirred in his arms.

"What's—?"

Cale covered her mouth with one hand. "Shh," he whispered in her ear. "Don't make a sound."

She nodded. He untangled their bodies and encouraged her to go behind him toward the open balcony door. The moment his feet hit the carpet of her bedroom, he pulled her close.

"Stay in here and stay quiet. The corner of the room, keep the bed between you and the sliding glass door."

"What's going on?"

He detected some fear in her tone. "I'm not sure. I'll be back."

She tensed.

"Okay, trust me, Taylor. I'll be back."

He could see her tentative nod because of his heightened senses and the moonlight. After one final, fast kiss, he waited for her to make it to the corner and sit. She wrapped her arms around her legs, drawing them close to her chest. He hesitated one moment and memorized her, hating to leave her but knowing he had to.

When the moon vanished behind a cloud, he ran to the balcony and launched himself over.

"Tiarnán!"

"New Order bastards. Coming around from the wooded sides."

He wasn't even going to ask how Tiarnán knew. It was like the man never slept. Cale snarled deep as he lengthened his stride, his weapons slipping to his hands. This was insane—they were attacking the house where his woman was. He would show no mercy tonight.

"Dracen?"

"Taking the back." Her tone was ice cold and he knew the men she came across would die.

"Aminta? Roz?"

"We're protecting your female and the children." Aminta sent the reassurance he needed.

He didn't respond. Didn't have to tell them she meant the world to him. Instead he focused on his upcoming fight. He moved stealthily through the forest, senses alert. The snap of a twig halted him. He pressed against a tree and bared his teeth. He could smell them.

Five approaching. Scattered formation. The weapons, their clothing. Them. All of it, he could smell. Flexing his fingers along the hilts of his weapons, he waited for the most opportune moment. Sure, they had guns and he didn't, but he wasn't fearful. Guns had a way of making someone feel overly cocky. These were his woods—he'd spent many hours learning and playing in them. No chance they would survive.

He could hear the whispers between them and held motionless as the first one moved by him. Waiting with patience he knew would make Tiarnán proud, Cale didn't stir until he was behind the man. Then he struck. Swift. Silent. Deadly.

Assisting the body as it fell to the ground, he ensured it made no sound. Then he set off on the next, even as he wiped his blade off on his pant leg. He removed two more with deft actions when a bullet slammed into his shoulder. Grunting, he dropped and rolled to a new position, angry at himself for being caught unaware.

Damn it. That fucking stings! He called on his power to heal him and set off after the one who'd pulled the trigger. His anger grew as he realized he'd been thinking about Taylor. *It's just like Tiarnán said, I wasn't concentrating.*

He could hear some faint cries from the other New Order fools and their communications grew murky between one another. His sign shoved him down and another bullet thunked into a trunk near him. This time he got it. *Sniper.* It was barely a millisecond later when the tree blew up and showered him with wooden, spear-like projectiles.

"We've got snipers. They're using some sort of exploding bullet." He sent the warning even as he took up shelter behind a different tree. Not that it would matter if the shooter launched another of those bullets.

Neither of them responded and he didn't take offense — not much got in their way when they fought. He flared out with his power and found the general area the sniper was located.

Using his speed, he ran for the hiding spot and roared with fury as he launched himself at the man. He'd been using night vision — Cale could tell from the green glowing eye around his head. That was the first thing he ripped off, plunging the bastard into darkness.

Still, his downward strike with his knife was blocked. This one wasn't a man off the street they'd given a weapon to. He was an experienced fighter. They exchanged punches and drew blood. In the end, poised to take the intruder's life, Cale raised his knife for the final blow.

"We need one for questioning." The male voice floated from the darkness.

Cale growled but lowered his blade and said, "This is your lucky day, fucker." Before the man could reply, Cale used his elbow and knocked him out.

"Are they all taken care of?" he asked, getting to his feet.

"Yes." Tiarnán pushed by him and hefted the man like he was a sack of groceries.

"Dracen?"

"Doing what she does." Tiarnán walked back toward the mansion. "You okay? I smell your blood."

"Fine. One of the bastards shot me. It's being healed."

His brethren grunted and let it go. Just like when they were younger, Cale felt bad, as if he'd let him down. They each had their strengths and Tiarnán's was fighting — it wasn't Cale's.

He fell into step with the hazel-eyed Guardian, and they made their way from the darkened woods to the open meadow before the mansion. Cale slanted a glance to the tall man beside him. The moonlight barely touched him — he blended in so seamlessly with everything, even when he was out in the open. However, he could see a bit. Chiseled features set in anger as his long strides ate up the ground before them.

He didn't take him to the front door. No, they went toward the back and a door opened silently for them, admitting them before slipping back into place with the same absence of sound. The hallway was dotted by floor lights that shined a soft amber.

The hall spilled out into a semi-circle surrounded by cells. With an impersonal touch, Tiarnán stripped the man down to his skivvies and tossed him in one of the cells. Then they took his clothes to a table and went over them, checking for tracking devices. The cell would sweep the man for any others on his body or in the final item of clothing he wore.

"What do you think prompted this?" Cale asked, dismantling a gun as Tiarnán worked on another one and Dracen walked in.

"I think with the re-emergence of the first artifact, yours, the creatures are itching for their chance. Since the rules state they can't come here and bother Lian, they have decided to see if they can get their human puppets to do the work for them and either capture the items, or flush us out," Dracen spoke.

Cale lifted his head to check out his sister. Her eyes were cold like Tiarnán's—nothing but business. Blood splattered along her skin and he knew it wasn't hers. Not even a scratch marred her black leather pants or tight leather shirt. She appeared every inch the warrior he knew her to be.

"Go be with your woman, Cale." She didn't even look at him, instead she stepped up beside Tiarnán and began looking over the impressive array of weaponry the intruder had brought tonight in the futile attempt to breach the mansion.

Setting the automatic rifle down, he nodded then headed for the door. A quick glance into the cell and he saw the man still lying on the floor, unconscious. He didn't pause, for the man didn't deserve his sympathy. He wouldn't have extended any to him outside had he been able to land a shot. Cale took the steps three at a time until he reached the first floor of the mansion.

Aminta walked around and when she saw him, she gave him a sharp nod. He returned it and continued his way up. Long strides took him down the hall to Taylor's room.

"Taylor?" he called out as he turned the knob and pushed the door open.

She remained huddled in the corner. Head resting upon her knees as she rocked back and forth. The fear on her face hit him harder than anything he'd done tonight. She looked at him, chin trembling. When he beckoned to her, she exploded up from her position and launched into his arms.

"Is it over?" she asked, holding him tightly.

"For now." He drew back and stared down into her face. With one hand, he hit a switch and turned on another light, offering more illumination so he could ensure she wasn't hurt. "Are you okay?"

"Shouldn't I be the one asking that? You're covered in blood."

"I'm fine, Taylor."

She gave him a skeptical look.

"Promise."

"The others? Are they okay as well?"

"All fine and accounted for." He moved his hands to her face, forcing her to use her arms and legs to remain locked about him. "All fine," he reiterated.

"Why did they attack?"

"Don't know yet."

"Yet?"

"We have one of them."

"Good," she said surprising him.

"Good?"

"They attacked a place which has children. Any of them could have been hurt. Good."

Cale brought his head closer for a kiss. It was official—he was falling in love with this woman. And it didn't scare him like he'd thought it would. Oh, he was scared, scared he wouldn't be able to protect her, but not because of his feelings. When she opened beneath him and her tongue met his, all other thoughts fell away. Nothing but him and her existed now.

* * * *

Taylor stood at the kitchen stove and watched as Roz whipped up a breakfast for the children. The woman was an embodiment of calmness. Personally, her stomach was still in knots from last night.

"Are you sure I can't help you?" she asked.

"I've got it." Roz deftly cut biscuits and placed them on a waiting cookie sheet.

Feeling as if she were a bit inadequate, Taylor scanned the room and went to sit on a stool. Roz looked at her and smiled gently.

"How are you doing?"

"Okay." Taylor shrugged when Roz raised her eyebrows. "I think," she amended. "It's different for sure. I mean, I've had my cousins after me for a while now and I guess…well, I guess it became natural and routine. Having armed men come at a big place like this is something on a completely different scale to me. What about the children? What about y'all?" Her accent thickened as her worry poured free. "Is this my fault? Because of Jeremy's association to this damn New Order thing? I should go."

Roz gripped her wrist. "One, this isn't your fault. This crap with The New Order group has been going on for a long time. A *long* time. Two, there's no way in hell the children were in danger. We were protecting them the entire time. There are safe rooms set up for them just in case whomever or whatever attacks get past us. Finally, no way Cale lets you go. You're not leaving, Taylor."

Her words somehow offered comfort. "I don't want to cause problems."

"Sweetie, our lives are problems. You're not causing any. How much do you know of what's going on?"

"Not too much."

Roz snorted. "Men. Always trying to protect women. This has been going on since the creation of the world. Lian has been battling them for that long."

It was a good thing Taylor was sitting down. "Lian? Lian is that old?" How old, she couldn't even begin to fathom. Alive since the beginning of the planet?

"I don't know how long the Earth was around before he showed up, but he's old. Look, I didn't want to believe any of this either, but since coming here, I've learned that there is so much more going on in the world than what we see with our limited sight. So much more."

Taylor stared at the youngest of the six and felt even younger than her. While she knew it wasn't the case — she had two years on Roz — Taylor felt like a teen next to her. "How do you handle it?"

"Handle what?"

"This...whatever it is that's coming?"

Her smile was soft and accepting. "The day Lian took me aside and told me more about my mark and what my destiny was, it took me a while to believe him. I mean, really? I'm supposed to be some sort of Astral Guardian? Me? A child no one else wanted? I was sure he was wrong. Look at me." She gestured at herself briefly. "I'm like, five-four on a good day." Her expression became amused. "Needless to say, I thought the man had lost his marbles. Then he brought in Billy, Dracen and Tiarnán."

"They were all here longer than you?"

"Yes. Cale and I arrived about the same time. And Aminta a year later." She went back to cutting biscuits. "It took some decent convincing on their part. Honestly, some days I still don't know what I'm going to contribute to the battle. But my path was chosen for me, years ago. All I can do is prepare to the best of my ability and be ready for whatever comes."

"And last night wasn't uncommon?"

"They've come before. Never when we've had an artifact though. And they meant business, being as armed as they were."

Her gut churned. "And you were out there fighting?"

"Me? No. I was at the house. Aminta and I stayed behind as an extra layer of protection for you and the children."

"I want to learn to fight."

Roz peered up at her. "What?"

"You heard me. I want to learn how to fight. When this shit comes, you'll need to be with the other guardians, doing whatever y'all will need to do. If I can fight, I can protect the children." *I hope, anyway.*

Roz's smile gleamed. "You know Cale won't be happy about that. He won't think you need to defend yourself."

"Tough shit."

"I knew I liked you." She nodded. "Okay, I'll talk to Dracen, she's the best to teach other than Tiarnán. And if we want to keep it from the guys"—she hummed and tapped the cutter against the counter—"best not to involve any of the guys in it."

"Not involve any of the guys in what?" Cale asked.

Taylor looked away from Roz in time to see him stride in, wearing a tight shirt and surfer shorts without any shoes on his feet. His hair was in disarray and had her thinking about what it felt like to slip her fingers through the silken strands. Grip them in her hands as he thrust deep, hard and… *So not the time to be thinking that.* Shifting on the stool, she gave him a small smile before glancing away to keep her true feelings from being noticed.

"A girls' night," Roz said smoothly. "Where we talk about men, favorite sexual positions and whether we prefer shaving or waxing."

Holy crap. Did she really just say that? Taylor watched Cale's reaction. Roz had said it so easily, just allowing the words to come free as if that's exactly what they'd been discussing, not about teaching her to fight on the down-low.

"Roz!" He held his hands up to his ears. "I don't want to think of any of my sisters doing that." He shook his head as if he could rid himself of having heard those very words.

Roz shrugged unrepentantly. "Shouldn't have asked, then. When you walk into a room and eavesdrop on a conversation, make sure you truly want to know, or don't ask."

"Could have lied and told me something else." Cale kissed Taylor briefly. "I so didn't need to have that mental image."

"So leave and let us finish the discussion."

He slung his arm around Taylor's shoulder and whispered dramatically, "Tell her, babe, you want me to stick around and that we should change the subject."

Taylor gave him an apologetic shrug. "Sorry, I'm really looking forward to finding out all this stuff. Shaving versus waxing and sexual positions is very important."

Roz burst out laughing.

"You two are wrong." Another kiss then he walked back to the door. "So wrong. I'm off to get that mental image of my sister out of my head. However," he said, winking over his shoulder at Taylor, "you can come discuss the sex positions with me afterward."

"You got it. I'll do research." Lord, she was proud she didn't melt through the floor with embarrassment.

Roz continued laughing well after Cale had vanished. "You're good for him. Don't back down, and give as good as you get."

"Thanks."

A gentle hand squeeze. "I mean it."

She knew she'd found a friend in Roz. "So, an attorney?"

While the remainder of breakfast was made, Roz filled her in on why she'd become an attorney. They were laughing like old friends as the foster children began streaming in for some food, followed by the older kids then the adults, who themselves were only a couple of years older.

She saw the respect they all had for Lian when he made his entrance. It went both ways. That was obvious. Not to mention his affection for them all. She watched him, taking this chance to observe the man who had done all this. No suit for him today, but slacks and a short sleeve button-down. Around his left wrist was a band of black leather, about two inches in width. And a wedding ring was on his left hand.

"Good morning, my dear," he spoke and it took her a moment to realize he was talking to her.

"Good morning, sir." She stood, embarrassed she'd not done so sooner.

"How are you settling in?"

"You have a stunning home and I'm settling in perfectly, thank you for opening it to me."

He flexed his fingers around the head of his cane and gave a brief nod. "My pleasure. If there is anything you need, don't hesitate to ask."

"Thank you, sir."

"Lian, please."

"As you wish."

A small grin, and he walked to the table then sat. Taylor helped Roz and a few of the children take food over and set it down. Although she was technically an outsider, they all made Taylor feel at home during the meal. The only one she didn't see—other than Billy, who was still in Scotland—was Tiarnán.

Cale left immediately after the meal and she stayed behind to assist in cleaning up, with some of the other children and Aminta this time. Roz also left, however, she left with a smile and hug for Taylor.

"Where's Tiarnán?" she asked.

Aminta paused in loading the dishwasher. Her dark eyes snapped around the room before returning to Taylor. "With the prisoner."

Her heart dropped like a lead balloon. "Prisoner?" How had she forgotten Cale had mentioned they had one of the men last night? And why had it been a good thing then and now...she wasn't sure.

"Yes. The one captured, the only one left alive from the attack last night."

She swallowed back her follow-up questions since two kids approached them with the remainder of the breakfast dishes. Taylor had no more opportunity to ask anything, for Aminta left with the children.

Alone in the kitchen, she sighed heavily and spun in a circle. It had been a rush yet presently there was complete silence. What was she supposed to do? Perhaps she could find someone who needed her help with something. Anything.

Shoving her hands in her pockets, she began to head to the doorway leading toward the living area.

"Ready?" a woman called from behind her.

She pivoted around and found Dracen standing there, expression serious.

"Ready? For what?"

"Learning how to fight."

A thrill skated up her spine. "Really?"

No emotion on her face, just a nod. "Let's get to it. Unless you've changed your mind?"

"Oh, not at all. I just didn't know when it was going to happen. Or if."

"Roz told me. We're all set up, let's go."

Anxious and more than a bit nervous, she trailed the woman who bore the sign of the dragon out of the door. This was it, she was going to learn how to fight. How to defend herself. How to kill.

Chapter Eleven

"Who's Blake?" Cale demanded, sitting in a chair as he stared through the bars at the man locked behind them. "And who's his boss?"

The man, standing in only his pants, shoved a hand through his bright red hair. "Go fuck yourself."

"No need to do that. Tell me what I want to know."

A sneer. "Or what? You'll send that brooding behemoth after me? The one standing behind you?" He gripped the bars. "You can't keep me like this."

"We are keeping you like this. And the one behind me, he's going to get you anyway. I was just hoping to keep it less messy. You don't answer me, you'll answer him." A shrug. "Either way works for me."

The chuckle wasn't so smug this time. "What is this supposed to be? Good cop, bad cop?"

"Not at all. One, we're not cops. But then you know that, don't you?"

"You're freaks," he hissed. "And let me tell you, The New Order will stop you and darkness will reign again."

"And you call us freaks," he muttered. "If you're so confident, why won't you tell us what you know? If you're truly as strong as you claim, it won't matter if we know or not."

"Where are the rest of my group? I see more cells. Trying to keep us separate so you can compare our stories? You can't stop us. More will come. You will be defeated."

He shook his head. "No need to keep you separate."

"Why not? None of them talked."

"Nope, they didn't," he agreed. "They're all dead."

"What?"

"You're the only one in here because you're the only one left alive."

"You can't kill people like that."

"Yet, you can trespass on someone else's property with the intent of killing them and whoever gets in your way?" His tone became hard as he thought of Taylor in danger again. "Not to mention, you're trying to plunge the world back into chaos."

"You're lying." He didn't appear as confident now.

Cale laced his fingers behind his head and rocked back in the chair so only the back two legs were on the floor. "For what reason? You want to see the bodies? I can bring in photos."

"Why didn't you kill me?"

He hooked his thumb in Tiarnán's direction. "He wouldn't let me. Said I had to keep one alive for questioning. Personally, I didn't care." He rolled his shoulders. "Don't think that puts you in a safe position, for he wants to kill you as well."

"Do your worst. I won't spill anything."

Cale sniffed and put the legs back down then rose. "Very well."

The man scratched at his neck. "Very well what?"

"You don't want to talk and I have no stomach for torture. I'm done here."

Tiarnán stepped forward.

"He, on the other hand, has no qualms about it."

"You kill me, you won't know what you want to know."

Cale's grin turned feral. "This is your mistake, thinking you have the upper hand." He stepped closer to the bars, where he could reach through and touch the bastard if he so desired. "Just because I said I had no stomach for torture doesn't mean I'm an idiot. And I see no reason to keep you alive because you may say something down the road. Like you said, more will be coming."

The prisoner's pale skin whitened even more. He moved his jaw and Cale crossed his arms. "Checking for that cyanide pill? It's no longer there. You don't get the option of checking out early. If we want to keep you alive, we will. If we want you dead, you're dead. You have no say in anything anymore." He checked his wrist. "I've wasted enough time here. Good luck."

"You will die, you hear me, you fucking bastard? You'll die."

"Not before you," he tossed over his shoulder as he left the room and headed for the stairs.

Cale took them two at a time. He truly wasn't into beating someone. He would do what was necessary to keep Taylor and his family safe, but if he didn't have to do it, he would just prefer not be there. It never seemed to bother Tiarnán. Or Dracen.

He wanted to find Taylor and hold her close. Allow her scent to calm him. Prove to himself she was okay. But he couldn't, he had things to do. Stepping through the sliding doors leading to the ops room, he smiled at Edmond who sat at the computer.

"What do you have?" he asked, sitting in a chair and wheeling it closer to the man.

Edmond's dark skin shined beneath the fluorescent lights as his long fingers flew over the keys. "I've inputted all the images from last night's intruders and have names for each and every one. Including the one who's still alive."

His British accent was thick and made Cale smile. Always had. No matter how long Edmond stayed here, he never lost it.

"Okay, so who are they?" Cale questioned. *"Tiarnán, Edmond has identified the men. Do you want to come see the information?"*

"No. I'm getting some myself. Will be up later on to compare what was divulged."

"Fine." Cale shook his head but couldn't drum up any sympathy for the man in the cell. He'd come looking to harm them. They were merely protecting their own.

As Edmond scrolled through the list, Cale shook his head over the range of people recruited. Rich, poor, all ethnic backgrounds and religions.

"I want to know who each of these people know, family and friends. Work acquaintances, everything. If they shared a latte one Sunday afternoon, I want the name of that person they shared it with. Somewhere, somehow there has to be a link connecting all these people. And when you find it, then we can go find this Blake person and perhaps move up the ladder of command."

Edmond nodded. "I'm on it already. Everything's being checked, cross checked and double checked."

"Thanks, Edmond."

"It's what I'm here for."

"And you do it so well."

"You know I love my technology."

"Very true, my man. Very true."

"Oh, before I forget"—he shoved away from his station and went to a different console—"I found this in the backpack, and the pendant, as well as the chain, are getting brighter. I don't recall gold ever shinning like this."

An image popped up in 3D over the desk and Cale moved his chair again so he could see it.

"It's like another link. For the necklace?" He didn't recognize it. "What's the symbol?"

Edmond nodded. "Yes. The symbol means rain. Thing is, this one is pure gold. I'm talking twenty-four karat pure. Soft and malleable. And the rest of the necklace and pendant, are now that."

Rain. He frowned. "Wait a minute. They're changing to pure gold?"

"They've changed. I ran a new analysis on them this morning. All of it, pure gold. You can see the dents from the creator's tools on them." He waved his hands around. "I don't know what to say. We have it as eighteen karat when it was first tested."

"How the hell…?" Cale was dumbfounded.

"That's not all."

"No?"

"Not even close." Edmond pointed to the screen before them. With a click of a button, he shrank the facial images of the men from last night and put up a split screen photo of the pendant—front and back. Correction, one was a photo still, the other was live video of each side. "Do you see it?"

He wasn't sure how the hell he would have missed it. Cale scrubbed a hand down his face as he got to his feet and approached the image.

"I've never seen anything like this before."

"Well, kind of new to me too," Edmond teased.

More symbols had appeared on the pendant. Front and back. The maze was still well defined, but in the center of it, where the maze paths went around it, sat a symbol he hadn't ever seen before, yet felt he should know what it was. The niggling belief lingered and it frustrated him he couldn't pull the information from his brain.

Little sparks, rainbow in color, moved along the labyrinth, hitting the different symbols then beginning again. His fingertips tingled and he had to stop himself from heading to the case and pulling it out to touch.

"When did this begin?" he asked.

"Not sure when. I didn't have video on the item itself. Just on the case in general, but it's not the right angle to see the back. When I checked it this morning I found it. I can only assume it had something to do with putting that last piece from the chain back within the rest of the links. As if it were the part that had been keeping it appearing as nothing more than a gold necklace."

"If The New Order finds out about this…"

"I know. And given last night's attack, we're thinking we need to move the case to the wall safe as well."

Cale sank back in the chair, fingers on his temples. "Sounds good. Do you have the urge to touch it?"

"No, not other than to inspect it and learn how the hell it's doing what it's doing."

"My body constantly wants to go to it and touch. Feel."

"Interesting," Edmond said, fingers flying across his keyboard again. "When did that happen?"

"When you showed me the video of the live feed."

"Makes sense, actually."

He frowned. "How do you figure?"

"You and Taylor share rainbow sparks when...things are...heated between you, right?"

"Not only then, but sure."

"That's more sparks. What if it's something that feeds your sign, your power? It would make sense you'd want more, crave more of it."

"Hell, Edmond, you may be on to something."

"I'm not just another pretty face, Cale."

He laughed and his tense body relaxed slightly. "Let me know if you find anything else out. I have to go talk to Lian."

* * * *

"You okay?" Roz questioned.

Taylor wanted nothing more than to curl up in a ball and cry. "Yes." She managed to force the word from her mouth. It still came out sounding like a wheezing person on their last legs.

"Positive? Because from here you look like shit."

That brought a grin to her face. "Thanks a lot." She readjusted on the bench and wished it were padded. Or like a cloud. Zero gravity. Memory foam. Just anything other than the hard wood it was.

"Not what you thought?" Roz joined her on the bench.

"Hell, no. I spent so much time on my ass, I think I need to sit on some ice. Or heat. How does it go, ice to numb the pain and heat to melt it away? I need something — she kicked my ass all over the place."

"Yeah, Dracen is a hard teacher."

"Couldn't have warned me?"

"I probably could have, but I thought to myself, if I told you, would you most likely want to back out? My answer was yes so then I went to something else. Let me think. Umm...nope."

Roz had a point. If she'd known it would be like this, Taylor never would have said she wanted to learn. "I feel like I was in the ring with a professional boxer."

"Well, she's professional. Don't think she's a boxer, though."

"Why do I get the feeling you're enjoying this?"

"Because I am," Roz whispered with a shitty ass grin. "It's been so long since I've seen anyone else look that way, normally it's me."

"Oh...you...and here I thought we were friends."

"We are." A blinding smile. "Just one of us can move faster than the other."

She whimpered. "More like one of us can't move at all."

"Now, now. Be positive."

"Trust me, I am quite positive. I cannot move." She coughed. "If I didn't think it would hurt me more, I'd fall over."

"Let me ask you something."

"Shoot."

"Did you learn anything?"

"Sure I did. Granted I can't move to use the knowledge, but I did learn something. Namely, don't piss off Dracen Lloyd."

Roz laughed again. "Come on, don't be a baby. Let's walk. You need to move the muscles so they don't tighten up."

"Move?" She sliced her gaze askew at Roz, her new worst enemy. "I don't know how I'm sitting upright."

"Come on. Up you get." She stood and reached out a hand.

Grudgingly, Taylor took it and winced when she was drawn to her feet. "Ohh, this sucks."

"Don't think about the pain."

"There's something else?" As much as she felt, she didn't think there was a way *not* to think about it. "Like what?"

"Nature. The horses. The children. Anything. Hell, think about sex with Cale if it gets your mind off how sore you are."

"As good as it is, I don't think I have the energy for that right now."

"There's always energy for sex."

"Is there?"

Roz winked. "Oh, definitely."

They walked slowly and Taylor would admit—not aloud of course—she felt a bit better as she moved farther along. They stopped when they saw Lian sitting at one of the outdoor, wrought-iron tables.

"Afternoon, ladies," he said.

"Lian," Roz replied.

"Good afternoon, Lian." Taylor wasn't entirely comfortable calling him by his first name, but he'd corrected her on it so she would go with that.

He looked her over from head to toe. "Drink this." He poured her a small cup of tea from the pitcher and added some herbs had with him to the brew.

Not wanting to offend him, she sipped it once she had it in her hand. The slightly bitter taste washed over her tongue and down her throat. Since the cup was so small, it didn't take her long to finish.

"Thank you."

"It will help," he said.

"Excuse me?"

"You have been practicing self-defense and fighting with Dracen. The tea and herbs will help your muscles recover faster."

She blinked, unable to find the words. How had he known?

Lian chuckled. "There isn't anything that goes on here I don't know about, Taylor Kenyon. Worry not that I will spill your secret to Cale."

She gave a short bow in thanks. "I appreciate it. Can we stretch that to not telling Dracen how badly I'm moving?"

His eyes sparkled with humor and he leaned closer. "She already knows." His words fell in a stage whisper.

Taylor groaned playfully. "Of course she does. Thank you for the tea. And the help."

"You are most welcome. Not to mention in good hands, learning from Dracen. Heed her words well, trust her advice."

"I will."

Roz bent over and brushed a kiss along his cheek then whispered something in his ear before they continued on their way. As they continued, as Lian promised, her muscles ached less and less.

"What did he give me?"

"No clue, some ancient herb."

"You knew he was out here, didn't you?"

"Yes. Figured you could use some help."

"The way I was feeling, I thought I could use a wheelchair. Or a coffin."

"Come on, let's go see my babies."

"Your babies?"

Roz broke out with a brilliant smile. "Yes."

They went to the barn and Taylor followed her inside and through the aisle toward a large door open in the back. Nodding at the children who were working in there, she kept up with the woman who had a fierce stride, despite being shorter. They made their way through a pasture to a fence that Roz climbed over. Taylor groaned.

"Come on, up and over. It's not that hard."

"Says the woman who didn't just get her butt royally kicked by some dragon warrior. I'm not sure who she reminds me of, but I'm sure it will come to me. Probably a mix of Rogue with her strength, Storm giving orders, Jean Grey when she was the Dark Phoenix and kicking everyone's ass because that's what she did me. And someone else." She snapped her fingers. "Oh, can't forget Shanna the She Devil. Right now, I'm going with an emphasis on she-devil. Extraordinary gymnast and athlete. Again, the ass kicking, you seem to have forgotten I just endured."

"Stop whining and start climbing." Roz practically bounced on the soles of her shoes.

Body screaming in agony, she made her way over the split rail fence then landed with decidedly less grace than Roz had. "Ouch," she deadpanned.

Roz rolled her eyes and went on her way. Taylor trailed after her, praying they didn't have to walk up that hill she'd noticed. Her muscles were better, not fixed. Thankfully that wasn't the way she was led. She still wished she weren't so sore.

They rounded a corner and Roz held up a hand, Taylor stopped and followed the finger she pointed with. Beneath a large oak were two foals and their mother.

They were dark brown with white blazes down their noses. Immediately awed by the cuteness, Taylor forgot about her aches and pains. The mare whickered and trotted over to them, the babies trailing after.

"How come they're not afraid?"

Roz grinned. "I have an affinity with horses."

Horse sign. Duh. They petted, stroked and played with the animals until the sun lowered in the sky. Taylor walked with one hand on the mare back across the pasture to the gate so she could avoid climbing over the fence again.

She smiled and shared a knowing look with Roz when they discovered a man waiting there for her. Cale. She clenched her fingers in the mare's mane to hide her own reaction. Shorts and a shirt worked so well on him. The backwards ball cap had him coming across as even younger than he was.

Cale swung open the gate as she said her farewells to the equines. "Have fun?" he asked, latching it again. "Hey, Roz."

"Cale. I'll see you later, Taylor."

"Thanks for everything." She waved at her friend who headed off back in the direction of the barn. "Yes. I did."

"You look a little sore."

"We were playing with the foals. They're strong."

"Come on, let me help you feel better."

Her nipples tightened behind her shirt and she had to struggle not to moan aloud. In her head though, she was dancing a jig. "What did you have in mind?"

"Bath and a massage."

The groan slipped free this time, for that sounded spectacular and incredibly enticing. "Let's go."

"First things first."

She stopped and looked up at him. "What's that?"

"This." He kissed her. His tongue swept through her mouth with dominance. In and out he stroked, before touching everywhere he could reach. When he broke away, her legs trembled even more.

"Oh," she sighed.

"That's one word for it."

She slipped her arm through his and he led her inside and up the stairs—more mental whimpering there as her legs screamed for mercy—to her room. He left her to undress while he started the bath.

"Ready?" he called out.

She walked into the bathroom wearing nothing more than her shirt, which reached mid-thigh. She carried some more clothing to put on after. "Yes." The aroma wafting up from the bathwater was soothing and relaxing. "What's that scent?"

"A mixture of white gardenia and spearmint." He glanced at her over his shoulder. "You're a bit overdressed for this, babe. And you won't be needing those clothes. You have a massage after the bath."

"I'm supposed to walk around naked?"

A wicked grin. "Works for me." One shoulder shrug. "In this room, anyway."

She removed her shirt, grateful the grimace came when the cotton was over her face, then dropped it on the floor beside the sink, which she'd placed the folded clothing on.

His gaze darkened and his nostrils flared. In response, her clit throbbed and nipples tightened even more. It was a heady feeling, knowing someone wanted her so much. Correction—knowing *Cale* wanted her so much.

"Climb in." His voice much deeper than it had been.

She walked closer, deliberately avoiding staring at the noticeable ridge in his shorts. Okay, so maybe she snuck a few peeks. "Thank you for this." Her own voice was huskier than usual as well.

"You're my mate. It's my job to make you feel better when you are sore."

She dragged her nails along the blue shirt covering his chest. "Are you staying to wash my back?"

"Don't tempt me. You're deserving a soak, so get in and soak."

"Or what?" She wasn't sure where all this taunting him came from.

He leaned in closer and put the tip of his nose to hers. "Or I fuck you against the walls and in the tub and you get even more sore."

She kissed him. "That could be fun."

He gripped her upper arms and swore. "No, this isn't about that. Get in the tub, Taylor."

There was no hiding the strain he was under to control himself and she let it go. "Okay." She climbed in, groaning softly as the heat penetrated her muscles. The heavy aroma sank in and when he put a folded towel behind her head, encouraging her to lay back, she didn't fight.

"Thank you," she said.

"I'll be back in a bit to check on you."

"Perfect," she muttered. This was heaven.

Chapter Twelve

Cale paced out in the bedroom, continually shoving a hand through his hair and doing his damnedest to keep out of that bathroom. She needed to soak — he could see she was trying not to show him how sore she was. They must have played really hard with the horses. He would have been concerned for her but for the fact she'd been with Roz.

Now she was with him. Naked. A room away. His cock pushed harder against the material of his shorts. This was not fair.

"I believe you said something about a massage."

He turned at the sound of her voice and promptly lost his breath. She stood there, a vision of loveliness. The steam from the bathroom hovered behind her in the doorway. The pink towel she wore wrapped around her, covering her breasts, and stopping mid-thigh. Her short hair was darker on the ends and he knew it was damp. She shined and he wanted to... Massage, he'd promised her a massage.

"I did." *Damn, when did my voice get so graveled?* "Come here."

She padded barefoot to stand before him. Large eyes watched him and he loved her thick, curved lashes.

"Lie on the bed."

"Stomach?" She paused. "Or back?"

Doesn't matter. I can fuck you either way. "Stomach."

She crawled up on the queen mattress and stretched out, arms by her sides. Her head turned to left so she could see him. In the depth of her gaze, he could see trouble lurking.

Willing his unruly cock to behave, he moved toward her and grabbed the oil he was going to use — the same stuff she put on her own skin after a shower. It might not be massage oil, but it would work in a pinch. He reached out and took hold of one end of the towel. A final prayer for strength left him and he pulled. The pink rectangle came off her body and he tossed it away.

Pouring some of the oil on his palms, he stared at her ass. Luscious. Plump. He wanted to bite it. *I have to focus.* He got to it, beginning at her feet and making his way up. Her occasional moans didn't help his libido. When he'd made it to the nape of her neck, she was limp beneath his hands.

He turned her to her back and stared at the woman laid out before him. Breasts high and firm, just begging to be captured by his mouth. Flat stomach, and hips he loved to hold as he thrust deep inside her. Her pussy hair was neatly trimmed and he wanted to sink his tongue within the lips and taste her thick cream.

Dragging his gaze up further, he met her eyes. They were dark and swirled with desire and lust, but she didn't move.

"Ready?" he asked.

"You're really good at this."

"I'll have to take your word for it." He began at her foot again.

"Why? Hasn't anyone else said so to you?"

"Never given anyone other than you a massage."

She smiled. "Glad to hear it. But then, how do you know what you're doing?"

"I don't. All I know is I want to touch you. Everywhere. Repeatedly. And make you feel good. That's what I'm going with."

"Mission accomplished."

Her legs were firm and moving up them brought him even closer to her slit. *Stay focused.* His current mantra.

"Glad you're enjoying it."

"I am."

He held her gaze and felt the reaction in his groin. So much heat, it nearly burned him. His hand faltered for a moment before he got himself back under control. He knew she was enjoying it, but he admitted to himself he liked hearing it from her as well. He could smell her arousal and that wasn't helping him any.

He worked up her left side to her breast then moved back to do the right. She moaned and shifted on the mattress. Taylor took his hand and slid it back down to her pussy, rotating her hips, grinding against his hand.

Cale got the message. The massage was over. Slipping back down her body, he nudged her thighs apart with his shoulders and spread her open. He leaned in and flicked out his tongue.

"Shit, yes," she moaned.

Up and down he lapped, avoiding her clit. One finger, followed by another, he sank inside her.

"Cale!"

Her heat wrapped tight around him and he wanted to be inside her with another part of his body. In and out he thrust his fingers, latching his mouth onto her nub. Her cry spurred him on. Nothing else mattered other than delivering her to orgasm. He grunted when she gripped his hair and yanked. Cale swapped his fingers and tongue, delving deep and taking all the cream she offered as she came. Her own honey poured on his tongue and he couldn't get enough of it. She tasted so damn good.

"I could do this forever," he said as she lay shaking beneath him.

"Inside me, Cale."

"No. I want more." He ripped off his clothing in record time. Lay on the bed and lifted her to sit on his face. "So much more." He groaned in pleasure, trailing his tongue over her folds.

* * * *

They ended up taking another shower together, later on that evening. Dinner wasn't attended and as they lay there, naked, limbs entwined on her bed, Cale stared out of the window. Taylor slept in his arms and he was perfectly content. Almost. If there was no threat he would be, but he was more content that he'd ever been.

"Billy? How are you doing over there?"

"I'm all right, Cale. How's your woman?"

"Doing well. Are you safe there?"

"So far. I've found a woman they've been tracking and am going to approach her about it tonight."

"A woman?" Cale heard definite interest in Billy's voice. *"Is she your mate?"*

"Not sure. Haven't talked to her."

"But you feel something."

"I'm a male and alive. An attractive woman makes me feel things."

"Deflection is always an option, brother."

"So is kicking your ass when I get back."

"I need a good training session."

"I hear your artifact is doing new things now."

"Yes." It wasn't a shock to him that Billy had been informed. Lian told them to always share information, don't leave the others in the dark. "It was freaky yet impressive. Still is. So what's she look like?"

"Who?"

"Your woman?"

"I don't know she's mine. She's just one they've pegged interest in. I'm obligated to help her."

"'Like I was with Taylor."

"Shouldn't you be paying her some attention?"

"I'm holding her right now."

"Go. Enjoy. I will talk to you soon."

"Stay safe, brother."

"You as well. Oh, I heard about the attack from The New Order. Is she okay?"

"A bit shaken up for a short time, but she's fine now."

"I knew she was a fighter. Later."

The connection vanished and he slid his lips along her forehead. She stirred in his arms and woke.

"We missed dinner, didn't we?"

"Yes." He took another kiss from her full lips. "Are you hungry?"

"I wouldn't say no to some sustenance."

"Let's go then."

They dressed and made their way down to the kitchen. It wasn't empty—Dracen and Aminta were in there fixing bowls of ice cream.

"Oh, so you do live," Dracen said to Cale. "We weren't sure when you didn't come down to fix dinner."

Oh shit! "I totally forgot it was my night. Who took it for me?" The look she gave him answered that question. "I'll take your next one, when is it?"

"Tomorrow."

Taylor buried her head against him and he leaned down to her ear. "What's wrong?" he asked.

"You were supposed to be cooking down here for everyone and instead we were up there…you know."

He grinned. "Oh yeah, I know. Trust me, I know exactly what we did. How often and in what positions."

She punched him and he captured her hand, kissing it. "Can you behave?" she admonished.

"I don't think so," he said. "Want some ice cream, or something more?"

"Ice cream works." She looked at the women. "What are y'all up to?"

"Watching a movie. Care to join us?"

"I'd love to."

Cale wanted her to stay with him, but he was grateful to them for including Taylor in their activities. "Is this a movie I'm invited to as well or is it women only?"

"You can come if you want," Aminta said, her lips curved up at the ends.

He knew that look. Holding up a hand, he shook his head. "No, no. You three go have fun, I'll find something else to do."

"You sure?" Dracen asked.

"Positive." He slid a bowl of ice cream to Taylor, who'd finally moved away from him to stand closer to Aminta. "I'll see you when your movie is over."

She gave him a smile that kicked up his heartbeat a bit more. "Sounds good."

He walked to her side, kissed her then left. Instead of going to another game room, he made sure no child was near then took the passageway down to the room where they had the prisoner. Tiarnán was already there and the man behind the bars looked like he'd seen better days.

"Has he spoken?"

"Yes." The deadpan way Tiarnán spoke sent chills up his spine. This man didn't mess around.

Cale thought about the woman who was destined to be Tiarnán's mate and prayed she would be strong. A weak woman wouldn't survive Tiarnán's intensity.

"What can I do?"

They both looked in the cell and the man cringed, afraid of what was to come.

* * * *

"Better."

Taylor would take it. Coming from Dracen, it was high praise indeed. Bent over at the waist, she sucked down air and balanced her hands on her knees. They'd been training daily, always at a time when Cale was occupied with something else.

"Thanks."

Standing upright again, Taylor looked at the woman she'd dubbed the 'dragon warrior' and shook her head. Dracen didn't even look winded. No sweat dotted her brow, her chest didn't heave in meek attempts to get more air. *Bitch.*

"You have good instincts," Dracen said, flowing toward her in a way Taylor was willing to admit she was jealous of. The woman was the epitome of grace.

"But?"

"You try to outthink yourself."

Hands on her hips, she tilted her head. "I do what?"

"You try to outthink yourself."

"Which means what?"

Dracen looked around. "When an attack comes at you, your body automatically begins to do something. Then, your brain gets in the way."

"So I'm harming my own training."

"Essentially, yes. You need to trust your body. Your instincts." She crossed her arms and braced her feet shoulder-width apart. "This last spar, what were the things that went through your mind?"

She moved her mouth like a gaping fish for a few seconds. "I'm not sure. I was waiting for you to attack then I was thinking…"

"Tell me."

She was embarrassed to admit it. "I wanted to impress you so you'd think I was making progress."

Dracen didn't respond for a couple of moments. "You are improving. What you need to remember, Taylor, is this is war. It's not a competition where you are going for points in a ring with observers. When you're called upon to use what you are learning, it will be in a life or death situation. Don't think about impressing me or anyone. Think about staying alive. Listen to your body. When you think about anything else, you try to do what you think I want to see you respond with. I don't care how it looks—if it works and keeps you alive, that's our goal."

She'd not thought about it like that before. "So, just because you showed me a roundhouse, doesn't mean I need to use that the next time."

"Exactly. I'll flood you with moves, help you hone them, but you, your instincts need to play a bigger part. This isn't a movie, there's no script here. And when you're fighting, there's no reset button. Some people are better with kicks than punches. Some vice versa. You have to discover your own talents, strengths and weaknesses."

"Discover my own weakness?"

"If you know it and are comfortable with it, no enemy can use it against you. A weakness isn't necessarily a horrible thing. You just need to know what yours are. Same thing with weapons. Swords are some's preference while the bow is others." A smile. "Like, I don't think I would give you nunchuks. Just a hunch. But a staff, I think you'd excel at."

"Who excels at the bow?"

"Roz likes to use the bow, but we all know how."

She licked her lips and rocked back on her heels. "Is there a type of weapon most don't use but you think would be a good one for me?"

Dracen crossed her arms and strolled around her. Taylor could feel the assessing gaze, but she didn't move, just allowed Dracen to continue with her study. She felt like a small kid next to Dracen, who just seemed to have her shit together.

"Honestly, I would equip you with an ASP."

She shook her head. "What's that?"

"I think a pair of them with clips so they could be hidden on your body. Collapsible ones."

She turned with her this time. "Which means?"

"Probably both sixteen to twenty-one inches." She placed her hands on her hips and nodded. "Yes. That's what I'd suggest."

"I'm still not understanding. What are you talking about?"

She waited for Dracen to fill her in on what all that jibber meant. The woman didn't say another word.

Taylor cleared her throat when Dracen walked away to a closed floor-to-ceiling cabinet. Standing as she was behind the woman, Taylor watched the impressive weapons display appear, only to disappear seconds later.

"Follow." Dracen strode off.

Mentally snapping a one fingered salute, she scrambled to keep up with the order. *Dragon warrior.* They went down to another level in the same room, a part she'd not been to before. *Been to? Hell, I didn't even know it existed.* The entrance was behind a thin bamboo wall. Beeping filled the air as Dracen typed in a code on a wall panel. There was a soft and faint *shink* before the wall beside the taller woman dropped back and slid to the left, vanishing.

Holy crap!

If she'd been under the impression that the amount of weapons in the cabinet upstairs was a lot, that had been a foolhardy mistake on her part. Up there, could be equated to an end cap at a weaponry store. This was like nothing she'd ever seen before.

Dracen led her toward the back from where a clanging sound emanated. The farther into the room they proceeded, the more her awe increased. *I don't think I've ever seen so many weapons in one place before. Hell, I don't think I know the names for some of them. Okay, a lot of them. Most of them.*

She increased her pace so as not to be left behind by the fast-striding dragon warrior. *Where is she taking me?* Her answer was received moments later when they passed through a large archway and entered a huge workspace. A forge in the middle gave out excessive heat and she immediately wiped the sweat from her head.

A tall figure stepped from a shadow and she had to hide her squeal of terror. The man was a behemoth. Jeans, boots and leather apron comprised his attire, while he had a huge sword in his hand. The gleaming blade reflected the flames and rested against his left shoulder. His arms were massive and she knew he'd be able to snap her in half without exerting any significant amount of energy.

Dracen didn't move and it was only with amazing fortitude that she didn't either. The man's face had a wicked scar, which ran diagonally across it, and he was missing part of his right ear. Her legs shook so bad she expected to fall into a pile on the floor.

"Dracen." His voice was deep and full of bass.

"Inaki." Her own was filled with affection.

Taylor breathed a bit easier when they embraced. Although it was more like Dracen was picked up like a rag doll and engulfed by a giant. But the woman didn't strike her as fearing for her life. When Dracen had her feet back on the ground, the large man looked at Taylor. She swallowed again and struggled not to show fear. His scar bisected one eye so it was nothing but a socket. His other was vivid green.

"Who's this?" he boomed, shifting the sword back and forth in his hand.

"Taylor."

She forced her legs to work and walked up to him, hand outstretched. "Hello, it's nice to meet you."

He looked a bit taken aback by her forwardness, however he recovered quickly and took her hand in his mammoth paw. It totally covered hers and she refused to panic. *That will be done later and in the privacy of my own room.*

"Inaki."

"A pleasure, Inaki."

He released her and instantly put his attention back on Dracen. "Why is she here?"

"She needs two ASPs, Inaki. Ones only you can make."

"She is mate to a Guardian?" Wonderment laced his tone.

"Cale."

Taylor stood still as his green eye snapped back over to stare at her. This time he paid a bit more attention. To what, she wasn't entirely sure, but she didn't move. After his intense perusal, he grunted.

What the hell did that mean?

"Come." He pointed to the floor before him.

She obeyed and looked up at the man who was clearly over seven feet tall. Probably closer to eight, but if she thought about it much more, she might faint. He gestured with his hands and she got the meaning. Lifting her arms out, she waited. He never physically touched her, just walked around her, but if she tried lowering her arms, he would grunt in a most disapproving way until she had them back where he wanted them.

He faced Dracen. "Give me seven days. Arms down," he added.

Taylor lowered them and put her hands together in front of her.

"Okay, we'll be back then." Dracen reached out and squeezed his hand. "Thanks." She jerked her head to the door when they had eye contact. "Let's go."

Taylor followed and didn't say a word until they walked out and the door closed behind them. "Who is that?" she asked.

"Inaki."

She rolled her eyes. "I got that. I mean, what's he doing down there and why is he locked in?"

"He's not locked in, that's where he works. Inaki is our weapons master. He makes all of what we use."

"He's made all of these?"

"Every last one." She smiled. "Amazing, isn't it?" She took the steps quickly.

"And he's going to make me an ASP?" Taylor tried not to breathe hard because, damn it, she wasn't that out of shape.

"Basically. Inaki takes ideas of weapons and fixes them with his own spin on them. Until he has them ready for you, we'll work with ones the cops use." They made their way back to the first cabinet and Dracen opened it.

"What are they?"

"This."

She caught the black cylinder tossed at her and stared at it. "What do I do with it?"

"Snap it open."

Taylor knew what it was now as the thinner part exploded out. A flexible baton. "This? You want me to fight with this?"

"Two of them." Another flew in her direction. "You can hide them on your person and they'll take down a man twice your size, if you use them correctly." Her grin was near feral. "Which you will."

At those three words, Taylor looked up and witnessed Dracen approaching her and she knew one thing for certain. This was going to hurt.

Chapter Thirteen

Cale stared down at the woman who slumbered on the bed before him. He'd just touched her shoulder when his phone beeped. *Fuck!* Checking the message, he saw it was from Edmond.

"What's wrong?" she asked.

"Edmond needs to see me."

"About?"

"I don't know."

"Want some company on the way?"

"Aww, babe, I didn't mean to wake you like this. I mean" — he grinned — "I wanted to wake you but in a much more pleasurable way."

She sat and kissed him before climbing off the bed and drawing on a pair of workout pants over the cute little boy shorts that had teased him. Taylor pulled on a cut-off shirt and ran a hand through her short hair.

"Let's go."

He smiled as he saw her footwear. A pair of soulful hound dogs stared up at him, their ears dragging on the floor.

"I don't want to hear it," she said, opening the door to her room and walking out.

"Adorable, babe. Utterly adorable."

She snorted and remained silent as they traversed the halls. His hand rested upon the small of her back when they walked in the room. Edmond sat at his usual place and he noticed that the rest of the room sat in general darkness.

"You called, my man?"

Edmond waved them over without looking away from the screen. "Sit."

Cale held a chair for her and caressed the back of her neck before taking the seat next to her. "How are you, Edmond?"

"Fine. Sorry to bother you. But I thought you'd like to see what I discovered."

The sound of his fingers tapping over the keys was the only noise in the room, other than the machines. He called up an image and Cale stared at it, immediately recognizing it.

"That's the pendant from her necklace."

"Right."

Beside him, Taylor straightened up a bit and he knew her attention had been snagged.

"What about it, Edmond?"

"So we have been so set on the symbols on the back here and the chain as well, I missed one."

"What did we miss?" Cale wouldn't put the blame solely on Edmond—it was on all of them.

"The maze. Labyrinth. Whatever you want to call it." He slapped the image up.

Cale stared between it and Taylor, who watched the picture on the screen. He reverted his gaze back to the enlarged snapshot of the pendant.

"Okay, so what about it?" He shifted on the chair. "What's it a symbol for?"

"Earth." Edmond pulled up documentation. "Mother Earth, to some cultures. But it's been in Crete dating back to three hundred BC, and other places as well. In fact, this is the symbol they believed was used to indicate—perhaps represent would be a better word—the labyrinth with Theseus. You know, the one built by Daedalus and his son Icarus on order from King Minos."

He gave a tempered smile, aware that the man tended to get lost in his research and dealing or working with his gadgets. "I know the story, Edmond. Does it hit anything else when you put all the words together?"

"A lot of phrases pop up, but honestly, I don't see how any of them affect us in terms of what is on the horizon. I'm not giving up, but it's slow going—there are a lot of different ways to use these words. I've linked it to the prophesy as well to see if it has any ideas that may hit off that as well."

"What's that one?" Taylor asked. "The one on the far left."

Cale looked as Edmond answered, "That's the symbol for The New Order."

"Does theirs have a meaning?"

Cale scowled at the three vertical lines, which were connected with a horizontal line. Flush across the top, however, the middle line hung down farther and had an empty circle at the end of it. "Yes," he said. "That's a symbol for Uranus, which has come to be seen as the destruction of the established order."

"Which is what they want to do."

"That and more, babe. That and more."

She fell silent again and he watched her for more signs of distress. Taylor was holding herself together remarkably well, considering. She rose from her seat and he shared a look with Edmond while she made her way to the special safe they'd had their weapons master build. Edmond had taken care of the alarm for it.

Her pants rode low on her hips and he had to catch himself a few times so he wouldn't be too distracted watching her walk. She had natural seduction down to an art form.

Taylor paused by the first case and reached out to touch the glass.

"Shut off the alarms, Edmond," he whispered, wanting to see what happened.

He gave a nod once it had been done. If Taylor knew what they were doing, she never spared them a single glance. She opened the see-through door, which wasn't glass but a tempered substance created to withstand not only bullets, but also what the demons could spit at them—their poison was a saliva that tended to act more like acid.

"Cale," Edmond whispered.

Tearing his gaze from Taylor, he looked at his friend and on to the screen he was pointing at. The man had put up the image from inside the container. The pendant had more sparks going than he'd seen and the gold was shimmering with a luster that made him think it was outside in the sunlight instead of inside under a box with a soft light.

"Has it done this before?"

Edmond shook his head. "Nope. It did that thing I called you down for and occasionally would start it up again, but nothing to this extent."

"Keep videoing." He rolled back his chair and walked to Taylor's side.

He slipped a hand along her back and kissed the top of her head.

"I never imagined it would look like this," she said.

"You wore it."

"I did. But it wasn't ever this bright or vibrant."

The sparks flared a bit further and became more active. Cale didn't understand what it was doing.

"Look at them," she murmured. "It's like they're looking for someone." A pause. "Or something. At first it looks chaotic, but the movements, once you stare at them, it's like they're methodically checking for something, that they need to complete whatever their purpose is."

He'd not thought about it that way. If she was right and those sparks were looking for the other artefacts…then this thing was about to blow up much sooner than they'd been thinking it would. It also meant Taylor was in more danger now.

"We need to talk." He sent the call to all then added, "Come on, Taylor."

He could sense her reluctance to move away from there, but she did. "What are we going to do?"

"I have to talk to the others, why don't you go to bed and I'll be in later?"

"Gotta do your X-Men thing, I suppose." She watched him for a bit, amusement in her gaze, then with a wave for Edmond, left the room.

"I like her, Cale."

"Me too, Edmond. Me too." It was actually more than that. So much more. He'd gone and fallen in love with her.

When the doors opened again, the others strolled in. Tiarnán walked in last, his face set in an impassive line. Staring at him, he wondered when he would see him smile more than once in a blue moon.

"What's up?" Roz posed the query.

He sat in his seat and waited for the others to do so before he started talking to them.

* * * *

Taylor walked around the lake. It was Sunday and the workers had the day off, so the vineyard was quiet. The children were doing their own thing and she'd slipped away for some time to herself. She needed to think. To reflect.

Snagging a place beneath some trees, she wrapped her arms around her legs and rested her chin atop her knees. With a yawn, she stared out across the smooth lake.

Cale.

As was typical, he was first and foremost in her thoughts. He had changed—he was still laid back, but not as much. Ever since that night in the ops room when she'd touched the pendant with all its sparks, he'd gotten even more serious.

"God, I'm pathetic," she muttered to the air.

During the day when he was off doing things, she would get her ass kicked by Dracen. It continued to hurt, but she knew she was improving. She had gone back to Inaki and picked up her weapons. The man still scared the ever-living bejesus out of her, but she hadn't shaken as much this time.

And he'd made two kickass batons for her. They were lightweight, but when she'd tried them out, she'd found they could shatter bone easily. Dracen hadn't given her any time to admire them though, immediately putting her back to work with them.

She wore them now. With Dracen's assistance, she'd tried out different places to have them on her body until she'd discovered the one that she preferred the most out of them all—against her pelvis, one on each side, angled so it never interfered with her daily activities. It was something she'd still not told Cale. Confused, she'd asked Dracen if she should. The woman had merely shrugged and said, "I don't know."

A snap from behind her had her turning. Nothing. Facing forward, she cast a glance up to the leaves to see if they were blowing. Nope. A calm, still morning.

All her instincts were screaming for her to get moving and get as far from there as she could. She rose to her feet and put her hands in her pockets.

"I don't think so," a man said as the barrel of an automatic rifle slid over her shoulder and pressed into her neck.

Fear slithered through her. She held still and waited for his next instruction.

"Sit back on the ground."

She nodded and slowly did so. The cold barrel against her flesh was so unnerving she wanted to puke. All it would take was for him to be jumpy or have an itchy trigger finger and she'd never see Cale again.

That thought angered her. It pulsed through her veins with every beat of her heart. Who was this fucker to take that decision from her?

"Who are you?" she demanded.

The barrel remained focused on her, but the man moved in front of her. A black bandanna around his head and his close cropped beard and mustache highlighted the harsh lines of his face. The black and green on it didn't help soften his appearance. His camouflage fit him well.

"New Order," she said.

"You've heard of us?" He showed her a perfect smile.

"Unfortunately."

His gaze narrowed. "No lip out of you. I'd hate to have to kill you before I get to enjoy your body."

"Why are you here?"

"We need the artefacts."

She shook her head. "What?"

"You're not one of the Guardians. That much is obvious, but who are you? Too old to be one of the kids he's taken in."

She thought fast. "I'm a teacher."

"So how do you know about The New Order?"

"Overheard some of them talking about it as I was closing up for the day."

He readjusted his hold on the rifle. "So what are you doing out here?"

"It's Sunday. No class." She gave him a reproachful look.

"You should have gotten a teaching job somewhere else, Teach."

"You could let me go."

"Not a chance."

Somehow she had to get him off guard. She didn't see anyone else, but knew if he was here, then there were others creeping along the grounds. A fierce need to protect it all filled her.

"Why not?"

"You're with them."

"I'm a teacher, I teach when and where I can get work. How did they get you?"

"The New Order knows who will be faithful to the cause."

"What's the cause?" She moved her hands and couldn't even describe her relief when the smooth cylinder of her batons rested in her palms.

"You know I served my country for years," he said gesturing her back to her feet.

"And?"

"And I know when someone is trying to stall." He narrowed his gaze. "That's exactly what you're doing." He no longer held the weapon on her, but off to the side.

She didn't respond verbally, just struck. With a singular move, she withdrew, expanded, and hit him with both batons. On the arm that held the gun. She knew how to break bones and she did that now. In less than five seconds, he lay on the ground, his right arm broken in two places, left wrist snapped and legs shattered at the knees.

Her chest heaved as she kicked his gun out of his reach and stood over him. "Leave my family alone. Y'all won't win."

His grin was ugly. "By now, they're close to the house. Why do you think we're attacking during the day?" Tears lingered in his eyes, but it was the smugness that bothered her.

"Why?"

"Because they're sleeping now." He spat. "Vampire scum do that."

She drew back. "Vampires?" With a scowl she shook her head. "Need to do your homework, man, or get a better boss. They're not vampires and they're sure as hell not asleep." She cracked him along the jaw and was off and running even before his head stopped rocking on his neck as he lay there, useless.

Why the hell did I leave without my phone? She berated herself as she hauled ass back to the house. Skidding to a stop as she came upon two more, she spun and flattened herself against a tree, heart pounding and lungs on fire from running.

They were between her and the house. Goosebumps burst out on her skin as she tried to slow her panic. She had to find a way to warn them. Perhaps she could head off to the left and circle around to the front, go in that way.

Now it seemed every step she made was loud and would surely give away her position. It sucked and her heart was in her throat as she continued to try to get through the line before it converged on the mansion. She needed to hurry. Picking up her pace, she thought she had got clear when a large, meaty hand grabbed her around the neck.

Holy hell! She'd almost stepped on him. The guy lifted her, his face a sneer that sent chills up her spine. Grappling with his lone hand that choked her, she gasped for breath as she hung there. He was big, not as big as Inaki, but large enough it kicked her ass to have his hand cutting off her air supply.

Spots flickered in and out before her eyes and she knew she was about to pass out. *No!* She couldn't do that.

Don't panic and remain calm. Dracen's words hit her and she sucked in the last bit of air she could manage then dropped her hands from clawing at his log-like arm. She grabbed one of her batons and snapped it open as she sent a swing right at his groin. As expected, he dropped her and himself to the ground.

Taylor landed on one knee while he fell fully, hands on his crotch and moaning loudly. Struggling to get air back in her lungs, she extended the other one and attacked. He threw a knife at her and it sliced along her upper arm, but he couldn't get up, for she'd broken his legs as well. Putting the batons away, she wheeled around and ran flat out for the house. The other intruders knew she was there as well and she had to warn her friends if she could.

Bursting from the tree line, she hauled ass over the manicured lawn. She didn't veer to go around items in her path—she jumped them. Stone benches. Hedges. All of them were hurdled.

In her periphery, she saw another rise up and turn his gun on her. She altered direction and began to run in a zigzag pattern.

"Cale!" she screamed at the top of her lungs. "Cale! New Order!"

The bullet slammed into her side, knocking her to the ground. She struggled to get back to her feet and found her legs wouldn't work. Clutching a hand to her side, she pulled it away and found it covered with blood. *Not good.* Using the ground, she dragged herself to the nearest bench and slid her body beneath it, opting for the best protection she could get for herself. People in camouflage poured from around the house. A siege.

A loud roar filled the air and she peered out in time to see Tiarnán slice the head off the man nearest him. The severed body part hadn't even hit the ground before he was on the next man with close to the same result.

She could see the others and another loud yell filled the air. *Cale.* She knew his voice anywhere. He jumped from a balcony and took out the one running up on him.

"Taylor!" he called.

More dark spots filled her vision. She tried calling out to him but didn't think her voice carried anywhere. "Cale. Cale!" Even from the distance, she could read his fury. And he held nothing back.

Her last image was of him fighting through two more, still hollering her name. Then her world went black.

Chapter Fourteen

He couldn't find her. Cale continue to battle through the endless wave of New Order fanatics that had come to the mansion. Each one he took care of, two more seemed to replace.

"Do you see her?" He asked the question to all his brethren who battled.

No one came back with an affirmative. Hearing her scream his name with such fear had nearly stopped his heart. The second time, when it had been followed by The New Order, he hadn't been able to move fast enough. He hadn't even had time to wonder how they'd gotten onto the property. All that mattered was getting to her and doing so in as little time as possible.

As fast as he was, Tiarnán still beat him. His brother in arms hadn't seen her, however, and had jumped into the largest swarm of attackers. Cale desperately sought her. Power raced along his skin and he listened to his sign, dispatching those who got in his way.

He reached a bench and crouched down. Beneath the large stone seat lay Taylor. The metallic scent of her blood reached him and he panicked. She was hurt.

"Taylor?"

She didn't move nor did she respond.

He stood and tossed the heavy bench off her. The sight waiting for him wasn't pleasant. She lay in a pool of growing blood, unconscious. For the first time in his life, he was torn. He wanted to fight and yet...

"Taylor's been shot."

"Get her to safety." Tiarnán sent the order.

"What about fighting?"

"Until she is safe, you will not be paying attention anyway. We'll handle this."

"Thank you."

Crouching down, he scooped her up into his arms then ran like hell toward the mansion. Bursting in through one of the side doors, he saw Lian waving him over.

"We have the operating room set up. We'll fix her."

He ran down to the room and placed her on the table. Lian wasn't far behind. The man washed his hands and looked at him.

"Hurry!" Cale snapped.

"Aren't you the healer?"

"I can't heal her." Cale touched her and the sparks began, surrounding her entire body so she looked like she lay within a rainbow.

"You are the healer, Cale."

Doubt assuaged him. "What if I mess it up?"

"Trust yourself. Do what you can until I'm ready."

So like he would for one of his brethren, he sent his power through her. Wave after wave of healing energy, all the while praying for the best. Lian was there shortly after and took out the bullet before stitching her up. Through the entire process, Cale continued to rest his hands on her, keeping her bathed in the rainbow sparks. To him it took forever, but he knew that wasn't the case.

"Done," Lian said, pulling off his gloves.

"Is she all right?"

"Yes. You need to trust yourself more, Cale. I will stay with her."

The sparks faded when he removed his hand. His power rippled and stirred. "Keep her safe."

Lian looked at him but didn't say a word. Just gave him a nod. Cale bent down then passed his lips over Taylor's and whispered, "I'll be right back, babe. Then we need to talk about you keeping yourself out of harm's way."

He ran with the same speed as he'd come in with until he was back in the last of the battle. Cale didn't take any prisoners. As far as he was concerned, everyone who'd dared to do this today deserved to die. And he would do his best to send as many as he could to Hell.

When he got shot, his sign healed him and he didn't slow. Just continued, hunting them down and killing them. He tracked one to the woods and as the assailant's lifeless body slumped to the ground, Cale turned his head to see another one lying there. The man wanted to move, that was obvious, but he couldn't.

Couldn't talk either, for the broken jaw. Cale could pick up a faint hint of Taylor's scent and knew she'd been the one who had done this. He crouched beside him, tipped his head to the side and stared.

"Got your ass kicked by a woman. A woman another of your men shot. My woman."

Aminta walked into view, her tiny body covered in sweat and blood. "How is she?"

"Safe now. With Lian." He gestured with his hand. "Taylor did this."

She didn't look at all surprised.

He stood. "You knew?"

"There are no blood injuries, at least not visible. He's bleeding to death inside, but she works with batons, so there wouldn't be cuts like we get. It makes sense."

"Batons?" How had he missed this? "Who taught her?"

"Dracen." Aminta stared at the man by their feet. "I know him."

"Dra— Wait, you know him?"

"Used to fly with him, occasionally. I can get him to talk."

"She broke his jaw."

Aminta's grin was evil. "He'll still tell me what I want to know." She bent down and grabbed the man's strap on his pack. "I'll take him. Go see your woman."

She walked off without another word, dragging the much larger man after her. Cale fell into step behind her. He didn't want to leave Aminta alone, but he had this pressing need to be with Taylor. So he ran.

She'd been moved to a different room and when he pushed in the door, he found Dracen and Roz standing there, staring at her. Both women looked at him, anger and strength on their faces. Without hesitation, he walked up to Dracen and kissed her.

"What the hell, man," Dracen said pushing him away.

Then he did the same to Roz.

"Aminta told me you trained her with batons. You saved her life. I found some men in the woods that she used the knowledge on." He turned to Roz. "And you. I know you were in on it as well. Thank you both, for seeing what I was unable to, that she had to be able to protect herself."

"You're welcome," Roz said. "Just no more kissing."

"You got it." Brushing by them, he went to the bed and saw Taylor lying there. Again, that strange stranglehold on his heart happened—like a fist closing over it. He rubbed his chest. Cale looked over to find he was alone in the room. He dragged over a chair and sat down to wait.

It took her a few hours before her eyes opened, but when they did he was right there. "Hey, babe," he said.

"Cale." She struggled to sit up. "The children?"

"Are fine. So are you, in case you were wondering."

Her smile was gentle. "Wasn't worried about me."

"I was."

"I have a healer to look after me."

"You sure do." He brushed some hair away from her face. "Can you not get shot again?"

"Not something I'd sign up to do on a weekly basis, that's for sure." She shifted. "So, did the X-Men prevail?"

He gave a snort of laughter. "Yes, we did. Despite my insistence, we're not mutants."

"Good." She relaxed again. "All's well then in the mansion." She held his hand. "Any thought as to how they got in and past everything?"

"We're running through the tapes. We would like to know what's changed to have them attack during the morning like they did."

"Easy," she said, gesturing for some water. "They think you are vampires."

He held the cup for her and watched her sip. "What? Vampires?"

"That's what one guy told me, not sure where he got that idea from."

"Me either." But it was a piece of information they could use. "I saw what you did."

"Hide beneath a bench?"

He stroked the side of her face. He could touch her forever. "No, to the guys with your batons."

She looked away and he guided her face so they could resume eye contact. "Sorry."

"Sorry?" He pulled back. "Why would you be apologizing for protecting yourself?"

"I'm not. I'm sorry I didn't tell you what we…I was up to."

"I already know about the women helping you." Another stroke of his hand. "And I've already thanked them."

"You're not mad?"

"Only at myself for not protecting you."

"Ah, Cale. You can't keep me in a bubble. Besides, in the grand scheme of things, being shot is minor. Given what is coming."

"You're so calm about this."

"What good will hysterics do? I flipped out enough when I met Inaki."

"You met him?"

"I did, he made the batons for me."

"Dracen." He shook his head. "That man always had a thing for her and would put her wants above all others."

"He scared the crap out of me, but I didn't lose it in front of him. I think I would have succumbed to hysterics earlier, had I not passed out. I'm good now."

"Babe, you're better than good. And when you're better, I'll prove it to you."

Her smile was sinful and he kissed her.

"Are you hungry?"

The flare of heat in her eyes had him adding another statement, "For food from the kitchen."

"Can Tiarnán bring it for me?"

He arched an eyebrow. "Is that what you want?"

"Yes."

"I'll tell him." He kissed her again. "*Tiarnán.*"

"*What?*"

"*Taylor's awake and wants some food from the kitchen.*" He could totally imagine the man's black eyebrow raising in disbelief.

"*You're telling me this, why?*"

"*She wants you to bring it to her.*"

For a moment, he thought he'd lost the connection. Tiarnán didn't involve himself in things like this and if he actually agreed to do it, Cale would be extremely shocked.

"*I'll bring her something.*"

Call him shocked. He glanced back to Taylor, who had reclined again, this time with a smug look on her face.

"You didn't think he'd do it, did you?"

"Not a chance in hell."

"I'm his little sister."

The confident way she said that warmed him. Tiarnán wasn't the most outgoing, but the two of them must have come to some kind of understanding.

"I'm sure that's it."

Tiarnán entered about twenty minutes later and the sight of Taylor's face brightening at the sight of him touched Cale. Their affection was mutual and totally platonic. He stepped back and watched the fiercest warrior of their six gently place a tray over Taylor's lap and kiss her cheek.

* * * *

Leaving the winery, Taylor waved goodbye to the workers as she passed them and began the trek back to the mansion. She grinned. The X-Mansion. No matter how many times Cale reminded her—and it was often he did so—they weren't mutants.

She snorted. "Not sure what label you'd give to a group of people who were each given extra-worldly powers and can do freaky things. Me? I call them mutants. Granted, Lian is far from being Professor X, but still."

The wind picked up, blowing little dust swirls around her, and she paused halfway up the rise. A black flock of birds rose from the forest and she gazed around. After a moment, she began walking again.

It had been two weeks since she'd been shot. Cale hadn't wanted to leave her alone, but she'd drawn the line at him accompanying her *everywhere.* Taylor paused and looked about her. She allowed him to do it for the most part, because she knew he held extreme guilt about her injury. She didn't blame him, but until he accepted that fact, she couldn't change his mind. Hell, the man would have cut up her food if she'd let him, then fed it to her piece by piece. This week he'd given her more breathing room.

Taylor continued on when the wind faded back to a gentle breeze. She took her time and picked some wildflowers on her way—they were her favorite. A mishmash of beauty that had it in them to survive in all elements, not something cultivated in a room under the maintenance of perfect conditions and temperature. No, these sometimes had missing petals or were drooping slightly, but it didn't matter, she loved them.

The mail vehicle was just pulling up the long, winding drive when she got there. She smiled and picked up her pace to meet the driver, waving as she stepped out.

"Hey! Afternoon, Haley."

The fit black woman moved smoothly as she took the steps with a packet of mail. "Hi, Taylor." She waved and jogged up the steps to place the mail in the box. "How are you doing?"

"Much better. What's new for you?"

Haley sported an excited grin as she came back to the truck. "I asked him out."

Taylor squealed softly and clapped her hands. "Really? That's awesome."

She and Haley had been talking since her second week here. It was natural for her to talk to the mail person—at her grandmother's that had been her one consistent source of human contact who was nice to her all the time.

"Tell me, what did he say? Who am I kidding, who would say no to you? Have you gone on your date yet? How was it? Is he a good kisser?"

Haley laughed and held up a hand. "He's accepted. We're going out next week. I don't know if he's a good kisser or not, but he looks like he will be." She went to the back and opened the rising door, the rattling sound familiar.

Taylor went back there and watched her pull some boxes from the back and set them on the bumper. "Where are you two going to go?"

More packages joined the others on the bumper. "Not sure. He won't tell me. Says he'll surprise me." There was disappointment in her voice.

"Are you not a fan of them?"

Haley shrugged. "Not usually. They don't typically end up well."

"Come on now, surprises are a good thing. Be positive," Taylor encouraged.

"Let me know how it works out for you."

"Huh?" She turned to see Haley step up behind her. Seconds later, a prick entered the side of her neck, informing her she was in trouble. *Get Cale!* She opened her mouth to scream, only Haley slapped a hand over her mouth, stifling it. Liquid entered her body as the syringe emptied.

"Don't fight it."

She wanted to but couldn't. Whatever it was, it was fast-acting. Her limbs relaxed, the stems falling from her hand and the weight of her body was supported by Haley. The darkness overtook her as she slumped forward.

* * * *

Her head pounded like a steel band was putting on a concert inside her skull, and she struggled to open her eyes. It was such a chore and she gave up, not having the energy.

"Don't get in my face, man. I succeeded where you and your men failed. You aren't my boss, Blake. Don't presume to give me orders."

Haley's voice hit her and she remembered the needle in the side of her neck. *Shit! She kidnapped me. Where the hell am I?* Taylor struggled again until she managed to prize off the chains holding down her eyelids. Not that it did much good. It was dark. A scratchy wool blanket that reeked faintly of moth balls rested below her right cheek. She lay on her side and since her arms didn't want to cooperate yet, she just used her eyes.

The cell, or whatever—wherever—she was in—was shrouded in darkness.

"Light that thing, would you?" Haley sounded frustrated.

A slight glow appeared, barely lurking around the corner, yet didn't approach further, however neither did it fade away. As she watched, it looked to her like it was dancing on the walls. *Damn drugs.* Peering up, she tried to figure out why she was in a cell. And it was an actual cell. Bars and all. She lay on a small—and uncomfortable—bed.

She returned her thoughts to Haley. *What the hell was she thinking? Why did she do this to me?*

The light grew brighter and she struggled to sit. As she did, she saw it looked like something she'd seen in some movies, where people were tossed into cells back in medieval times. Old.

Two people came around the corner and she had to blink a few times. Haley carried a torch. *Are you kidding me? An actual piece of wood with fire? No lantern or oh...electricity to turn lights on?* What kind of mess had she fallen into?

"What did you do to me?" she demanded, hating her scratchy voice.

A tall man, fit and well-dressed, stepped past Haley and stared at her through the bars. It took a few seconds but—to her incredible surprise—she recognized him. He knew it too.

"Hello, Taylor." His voice continued to have the power to make her long for a shower.

Flashing her gaze between them, she desperately tried to make sense of the entire situation. "You? You're Blake?"

He grinned, the light glinting off his gold teeth. "You remember me? I'm honored."

"I don't forget assholes," she snapped. He'd been a small time loan shark who'd often dragged her cousins into his clutches. They'd gone to their grandmother to either get money from her or to steal something to pay him back.

"So sassy. Not so proud now, are you? I wanted you so bad, but you would stare at me like I was the scum of the world. Like you were so much better than me."

She lurched unsteadily to her feet and stumbled to the bars as her legs thought about working properly. Clutching the bars, she made sure to hold his gaze.

"I could be living in the sewers and I would still look at you like you're scum, because you are. Nothing is going to change that." Dismissing him, Taylor turned her attention to Haley. "What did you do, Haley?"

The woman stepped closer, the light from the torch glinting off her hard, dark-brown gaze. "I did what no one thought I could do. I got the one who brought the first pendant." Her grin was pure evil. "If they want you back, or rather, if *Cale* does, they'll trade the item for you."

"They won't trade for me. You'll never get the item. How did I not know?"

She laughed. "No one did. Not even the *Guardians* knew. I had access to your place daily and you just made it so easy for me."

"They'll know you took me."

"Not a chance, Taylor. I stuffed you in the back of my vehicle and even went back to put packages down. You forget, I was there every day. I know how and where to park so no camera can have access to the back of my vehicle. And tomorrow, I'll go back again."

Her face twisted in an ugly mask of pleasure. "I even picked up your flowers you picked and threw them away after I left the grounds. You're here for the duration, may as well settle in and get comfortable."

She wanted to cry and curl up in a small ball. Instead, she adopted a sneer of her own. "I don't think so."

"You just said they wouldn't trade for you. If they don't think we're serious, we send body parts until they know we are."

Fear grew in a large knot within her stomach. She ignored it. "I said they wouldn't *trade* for me. I never said they wouldn't come for me. Cale loves me, he'll be here and *when* he gets me out...I'm coming for you."

Her blustering bravado must have had some effect, for Haley's expression held a flash of fear. Blake's as well. Haley hissed some obscenities at her before stalking away, leaving Taylor in the dark. Carefully, she made her way back to the bed and sat on the inch thick mattress, if she could call it that. More like piece of foam.

Scooting back until she rested against the cold wall, she hugged her legs and rested her chin on her knees.

Please find me, Cale. She didn't know if he loved her or not. She hoped so, but there wasn't anything concrete she could hang her hat on in that venue. He would protect her and that was her single ray of hope shining through the darkness in her soul. Cale would come for her. He would. Maybe not for love, but he would come, she held on to that ideal.

Chapter Fifteen

Cale paced. Where the hell was she? This wasn't like her, not at all.

"Anything?" He sent the question out to his brethren who were assisting him with the search.

Unfortunately, they all sent back a negative response. He ran his hands through his hair some more while he paced back and forth outside the front door. Soon the other four Guardians stood with him outside. The lights shined down on them all, highlighting the worry in their expressions. All aside from Tiarnán, who was as readable as a brick wall.

"I don't know where she could be." Fear was growing swiftly inside him. "All her stuff is in her room. None of the kids have seen her. In fact, the last ones to see her were the ones at the winery, she'd spent time down there earlier."

"What about her cell?" Roz asked. "Can we track her that way?"

He shook his head. "It's in her room."

I'm not letting that woman out of my sight again!

"None of the vehicles are gone, do you think she just took a long walk off the property and got tired? Settled down to rest and fell asleep?"

"I don't know, it doesn't seem like her, but I'll check off the property." He wanted to scream his frustration to the heavens. "Thanks," he muttered, jogging to his car. It didn't surprise him in the least when Tiarnán clamped a hand on his shoulder, halting him from entering his vehicle.

"I'll drive, you search."

Moments later, they rolled from the vineyard in Tiarnán's truck. Night had long past fallen and it wasn't easy to see as the thick cloud cover didn't allow for much of the moonlight to sneak through. His frustration grew as time ticked past and they remained unable to find a single sign as to where she had gone.

They drove back up the drive at three in the morning. Cale was tired and pissed. Tiarnán didn't try to stop him when he jumped out and strode inside without waiting. He wished Billy were here to talk to. Cale made his way back to her room and checked it one more time, although he already knew what he'd find. Her things, but not her.

Thunder rumbled off in the distance and he walked out to her balcony and leaned against it, fingers curved into the wood as he struggled not to lose it. The wind picked up and the clouds overhead began moving at a much faster pace.

"Storm's coming."

"Do you know where she is, Lian?" He didn't even face the direction the voice had come from, knowing Lian would be in the darkest part.

"No."

Now he turned. Lian was a man who relished giving them riddles and making them figure things out on their own. The rapid way he answered concerned him. Sure enough, the man stood in the corner, hands braced upon the top of his cane.

"That's it? Just *no*?"

"I know you wish this was a test and I want you to figure it out, but I don't have any idea where she is. Who she is with is another thing entirely. But her location, I haven't a clue."

"The New Order took her."

"We've had contact!"

Aminta's voice burst into his head and without hesitation, he ran for the ops room, Lian following behind him. All but Billy were in there. Edmond sat in his usual spot, fingers flying across the keys.

"What happened?"

"They made contact. Pulling up the video now." Edmond didn't stop while he updated what showed on the screen.

Cale's heart seized painfully at those words. Video. He sat in a chair, knowing his legs may very well give out on him if the images were bad.

"Here we go," Edmond said.

An image popped up and he leaned forward. *Taylor!* She lay on a thin cot, curled up in a ball.

"As you can see," a computerized voice said. "We have something we think you'll want. You have something we want. So we're proposing a trade. The pendant and necklace for the girl. You have five hours to come up with an answer and will be contacted then. You say yes, we'll set it up. You say no and she gets to spend the rest of her life—which wouldn't be that long, although would seem like an eternity to her—with us."

The camera zoomed in on Taylor's face and his gut clenched at the sight of dried tearstains on her cheek. Rage unfurled and spread throughout him.

"Five hours."

The voice and the image disappeared.

"Where is she?" he demanded, glaring at Edmond.

"I don't know. I can't pull up anything on them which would tell location." He shook his head in frustration. "I'll keep working on it, though."

"Play it again," Tiarnán said.

He didn't want to see it. "Why?" Cale demanded.

"So we can see if there are any recognizable things in the background." Tiarnán never raised his voice, maintaining his usual tone.

"I taped it in case it was something that would disappear once it had been seen," Edmond said. He pressed a few buttons and it popped back up on the screen. This time, the image was much larger. Still mostly dark, just a soft light in the background.

"Can you lighten it any?" Tiarnán and Dracen asked simultaneously as they moved closer.

"Not much, but a little."

Cale watched as it got a bit brighter on the screen. He could see bars now. They were holding her in a cell. A fucking jail cell. His fury thickened and he forced himself to remain still and not break the table he was at. He rose and went to gather closer as the others did. No one offered him any words of comfort and he was glad. They couldn't possibly know what he was going through.

"It looks old. That one stone there by her head, this isn't a modern cell." Roz tapped the part she talked about. "They don't have rough walls like this now. Plus, look at the top by the bars on the cell, that's old mortar."

"So we're looking for an old prison?"

Cale couldn't keep his eyes off the woman lying there. She was everything to him and if they didn't play it right, he'd never have the chance to tell her so. "Wait," he said.

The video paused. "What?" Dracen asked.

"Edmond, zoom in near her hand, by the floor."

A few clicks and it was done. Sure enough, he hadn't been seeing things. She had written a name in the dirt floor. *Blake*.

That was all he needed to see. Cale whirled around and ran from the room, his rage pushing him along. Outside the windows he ran past, lightning flashed and rain began pelting the glass. He didn't slow, taking the stairs down in almost two jumps.

With a feral growl, he strode into their prison and holding area. Two men were in there. One nursed a broken jaw and the other looked like he'd gone rounds with Ali in the ring.

They looked at him.

"Here's the deal. The first one who talks I let have a much easier time."

They narrowed their eyes at him.

"Who's Blake and where the hell do I find the fucker?"

Both glanced away and he snarled at them, getting them back to looking at him.

"Don't make me ask again." He stared at Broken Jaw. "I know you can't speak, but you can write. So write it down."

The man shook his head defiantly.

"You thought we were vampires, if you don't tell me what I want to know, you'll *wish* I was one."

"What's the matter, man? Lose your woman?"

He whirled on the man. "What do you know?"

"More than you," he taunted. "Every step you make, we're already ahead by six. You'll not get her back unless you do as they say." A shrug. "Maybe."

He stepped to the bars and glowered at the man in there with his smug expression. "You."

"Me what?" he asked crossing his arms.

"You, you get my attention."

He scoffed. "You don't like torture, remember?"

Cale opened the cell door and stepped into the small space. "That was before your New Order fuckers dared touch my woman." The door clicked behind him, locking them in there together. "Now it's you…and me, until someone else comes to open the door."

The man's eyes widened and he took a step back. Power flared and Cale crossed his own arms.

"Wh-what do you want?"

"I want to know everything you do. And we will begin with the man named Blake."

"I told the other one all I know."

"You'd better tell me something more." Another step.

"What are you doing, Cale?" Tiarnán sent the question.

"Getting answers."

"Okay."

"He is connected to them somehow. He knew they'd taken Taylor."

"Are you sure?"

"He just told me."

"I'm sending Dracen."

The connection ended and he met the man's gaze. Now it seemed more fearful.

"Tell me where I can find Blake."

"No way, he'll kill me."

"So you're not that important to The New Order, then."

He puffed out his chest. "I am."

"Right." He backed him into a corner and put a blade to his throat. "I know and you know that you have some way of contacting them. Some mental thing? I don't know how, but next time you make a connection, you tell those bastards I'm coming for them." He leaned in close. "And when I get there, there will be hell to pay for daring to come after her." His voice fell in a low growl and a line of red began to coat the metal blade.

"*Let him go, Cale,*" Dracen said.

The door opened and he saw her step in. The door stayed open, but he didn't move from the man.

"*Cale.*" It was a warning. He listened this time, removing the dagger and stepping away.

"*What are you going to do?*"

"*We all have our gifts, Cale. Leave us.*"

"*I'm staying.*"

No way they would push him out. She may be older than him, but, damn it, Taylor was his mate. No one else's.

Mist filled the area as she walked by him, blocking the majority of his view of Dracen and their 'guest'. The man's gut wrenching scream was such that it sent chills up Cale's spine. It began and it was done. The mist faded as Dracen moved back toward him.

"What happened?" He didn't know much about what her powers were—she didn't talk about them much, just fought.

"I found out who Blake is and where he lives."

Falling into step behind her, he cast a glance at the listless man crumpled on the bed. His eyes were glassy and unfocused as he stared off into oblivion.

"He dead?"

"No. He'll wish he was though, when he comes to."

They secured the cell door and took off at a run. One good thing was that he was always ready, for he carried his weapons with him. Pushing outside, he was instantly soaked.

"Be safe." Lian's blessing came down.

He dashed through the rain to the helicopter on the landing pad. It was running and he knew Aminta was behind the controls. He hopped in and she lifted off.

"We will be there, Cale," Dracen said as the chopper shot forward and continued to gain altitude.

"I'll let you out about fifteen clicks away. Then you're on your own. Edmond showed the security, it's impressive so we'll be picked up if I get closer than that. Right now, I'm just a police chopper out."

"We sure she's there?" There was no need for headsets with Aminta, not when they could communicate mentally.

"No, but Blake is. Or was when Dracen sent the information. Edmond used his computer's camera to see and spied him."

"And we know it's him?"

"Since some bimbo came in the room and called him such, he's confident." Aminta fell silent and didn't speak again for ninety minutes—they left the rain and flew through clear skies. "Once you land, head due North. Chase the storm."

He flexed his fingers, calming a bit at the cool feel of metal in his hands. When Aminta dropped equal to the tree line, he gave her a small wave then leaped out to the ground. He dodged to a tree and hid as she rose and veered away.

Once it was only him, he headed due north as she'd instructed, using the speed and senses he'd been given. Around him, the night was still calm. Where he was heading, the storm had already arrived. Chasing the storm was precisely what he was going to do, and he had less than three hours to get her out of there. He had no intention of failing.

* * * *

Taylor tried to get comfortable. It was damp and smelled musty. She'd since erased the word she'd written in the dirt, not wanting them to think she was doing anything.

Haley walked into view, a tray in her hands. More than one torch offered illumination now, yet none were actually in her cell.

"Food. Eat." Haley slid the tray under the bottom cross bar of the cell.

"Why are you doing this, Haley?"

"Because it's time for a change. I've dedicated my life to The New Order." She drew out her lower lip and showed Taylor the brand on the inside. Then she grinned. "I was born to the Order."

"Born to it? What do you gain from this?"

"Besides the power and wealth I was promised?"

Taylor's face must have conveyed her doubt.

"You're sitting there thinking they're using me and I'm expendable. I'm not."

She had been thinking that. "What makes you so special?"

"My father."

Dread welled up. "Your father?"

"Yes. He's one of the beings your friends want to kill and defeat." Haley shook her head, eyes burning an eerie red. "I won't let it happen. We won't."

"Who's your father?"

"Hara."

She filed the name away and walked to the tray. Unappetizing. Gloppy and congealing. She lifted the tray, frowning at the sight of a cream plastic spork. *Seriously? A spork? Guess I'm not tunneling out of here with this.*

Haley watched her and eventually Taylor turned her back and returned to the bed. When she sat and peered out through the bars, Haley had vanished. Only leaving her with light from one torch.

She pushed the tray away and began to investigate her cell. There had to be some way out of this old place. Cold, damp rock. No window. She checked the bars then returned to the bed and lay on her stomach. *How the hell am I getting out of here?* Pressing along the corner, she paused when the stone shifted.

If I could get out...

Taylor altered her position and grunted when something jabbed her in the ribs. *What the...?* She could have smacked herself in the head. *Christ. My batons.* She had weapons. *How did I forget I carried them?*

Feeling immensely better, she blew out her breath and calmed down. She was armed. Now to plan her escape. After moving the tray back nearer to the bars, she returned to the bed. She faced the corner and slipped one weapon free. Extending the baton, she began to dig along that loose block.

Occasionally, she would shake her shoulders as if she were crying. When she heard someone returning, she retracted the baton, adjusted the blanket to hide any mortar that may be noticeable under the cot, and faced the bars, wiping at some imaginary tears.

Haley again, and someone else with her.

"They aren't going to trade," Taylor said, lifting her chin.

"When we begin to send body parts, I'm sure they will reconsider." Haley spoke as if talking about a summer's day picnic. As if she actually looked forward to sending the parts.

Body parts? Had she even attempted to eat the nasty crap on the tray, it would have been regurgitated with those two words.

She pushed to her feet and stalked to the bars. "You bitch! I thought you were my friend."

Haley sneered and stared down her nose. "You were supposed to think such a thing. That's why it worked."

Taylor kicked the tray at her, getting a small measure of satisfaction when a plop of it landed on her boot toe. A very small measure, for Haley barely acknowledged it.

"We'll see how brave you are."

Fear lifted its head and she swallowed hard. "Do your worst." She might be about to die, but she'd be damned if she gave these bastards any satisfaction of knowing how scared she was.

The man beside Haley stepped forward and reached through the bars. He lifted his hand and her entire body rose along with it. *Shit!* The bars melted at his touch and he walked in, bringing her close. Behind him, the bars repaired themselves.

"You"—he sniffed her—"smell like fear and that pup, Cale."

"Are you Hara?"

His laughter was extremely unpleasant.

Every part of her, on a visceral level, tried to pull back from him. It hurt—his laugh hurt.

"No. I am Tryvek."

"Demon?"

If his laugh had been bad his smile…worse. Pointed teeth were bared to her, yellowed and rotting. "No." He brought her closer.

Her eyes burned from the stench rolling from his mouth. "What are you?" Did she really want to know?

"The punisher."

Her mind flashed to the DC Comic character and she immediately realized she'd rather meet the DC one.

I will not panic. She repeated that numerous times. Haley had left. Taylor located her batons and palmed them. "Am I supposed to beg for mercy from you?"

"If you want. Please amuse me, but"—he began to eliminate her air supply—"it will do you no good."

He used his other hand, wrapped in a black glove, and reached to her face. She wanted to pull away but remained defiantly motionless. Her lack of movement was only exacerbated by the fact she still struggled to breathe. He stroked her cheek.

"Such beauty. We will have such fun together."

"Doubt it," she gasped.

"I am going to enjoy you."

Breathing as normally as could be expected given her situation, she waited a couple of seconds more. Then attacked.

She went after his knees simultaneously. They both fell to the ground, however as she'd known it was coming, she landed on her feet while Tryvek howled in pain. Taylor didn't hesitate—she *had* to keep him off guard. She launched another attack.

The batons whipped through the air, striking him with blow after blow. He grabbed the end of one, inches from his temple. He hissed something she didn't understand but nothing happened. She struck with the second one as he jumped up.

"Who made those?" he demanded, coming at her again.

He backhanded her. Stars exploded as she whirled away to land, roll and rise again, ever so grateful for all the beatings she'd gotten during training with the dragon warrior. Tryvek didn't slow either, and he was on her with swiftness. His massive fists delivered punishing blows. She weakened while he didn't.

Outside the bars, demons had arrived and were screaming and grabbing at the metal with their feet and the claws at the tops of their wings. Chest heaving, she waited for his next attack. Deflecting his first swing, she allowed him to grab her and lift her so they were eye to eye. She was out of options, this was her final play — she just couldn't keep up with him.

Using her waning strength, she shoved her other baton straight into his eye and beyond. He fell like a rock and took her with him. Something snapped in her arm and she cried out.

The screams from the demons got louder as more gathered. She pushed away from the still form of Tryvek, cradling her arm. Circling him wide, she put his body between her and the cell door. They fell quiet as she put away the first baton and went to the one sticking out of his skull.

Thick, green liquid — pea soup green — ran down his face from his eye. The noxious smell turned her stomach. Grasping the handle, she glared at the demons, who for some reason couldn't — or wouldn't — come into the cell. Then she jerked the baton free. More green dripped from the end mixed with some gray. She flicked it at them, causing them to scramble back.

Don't want to touch it. Her legs shook and she backed up to the bed, knees buckling when she bumped the frame. She found it nigh on impossible to look away from Tryvek. Had she killed him? And why was it so hard to breathe?

Spots appeared before her eyes and she slumped to the side.

* * * *

"I want her dead!" An angry statement, which penetrated the blanket of nothingness that had surrounded her.

"If we kill her now, we have no bargaining chip." Male voice. Blake, if she was right.

"I don't care. She *killed* Tryvek!" Possibly Haley? The tone was so high it was hard for her to decide.

Taylor opened her eyes and tried her best not to scream in pain. She lay on an elevated table, arms over her head, cuffing her there. The broken arm didn't like the position. Her legs were also secured in the same fashion. To her right stood Haley and Blake.

He noticed her first. His grin widened and he moved toward her. He picked something up and showed it to her. Her baton.

"Where'd you get this?"

"Present." It was difficult to talk. Her throat was so dry.

"From?"

She closed her eyes only to open them when a sharp pain went in her shoulder. Haley had stabbed her.

"You bitch! You killed Tryvek."

Her lips were busted and swollen, still, she smiled best she could. "Did the world a favor."

Hatred—quite possibly too mild of a word—filled Haley's features as she turned the blade. Taylor screamed, unable to contain it.

"Haley, Lamar won't be happy if she's dead."

"I won't kill her. Yet."

More screaming came courtesy of the pain she endured. Tears streamed from her eyes as Haley picked a few more places to put the knife.

Blake didn't say anymore, just leaned against a wall and watched.

"What was that?" he broke in after numerous cuts.

Haley looked at him. "What?"

"There was some sparking by her fingertips."

Haley turned back and shrugged. "Don't see anything."

Taylor drifted in and out of consciousness as her pain threshold was surpassed. She moved her head to peer up at her fingers, praying for a spark.

Cale.

A wave of them alighted along her fingertips.

"Did you see it?" Blake approached, pointing.

"Shut up, Blake, before I decide to kill you."

I didn't imagine it. Cale, please. Hurry.

The knife sank in again and she welcomed the pain-free darkness.

Chapter Sixteen

Cale ran like he had everything to lose. He did. Taylor Kenyon. Drawing on every drop of speed his power gave him, he nearly flew through the trees and covered those fifteen clicks in a short time. In tune to his sign, he slowed at the trickle of warning it gave him.

Overhead, he noticed he'd caught up to the storm. Thunder rumbled and deadly lightning jagged through the clouds. He climbed a tree and scouted the area. The house was surrounded by armed guards and dogs were patrolling the perimeter.

He spied a small, unmarked door on the first floor and looked up from that position. There was a way for him to get in the building. Leaping to the ground, he landed then took off again. When the skies opened up, he went back up in a tree and waited as the closest patrol went by him.

Sprinting through the grass, he listened to his sign as it directed him around booby traps. It took him seconds to pick the lock and slip through the door.

"I'm in his house."

"We're almost there." Tiarnán didn't tell him to wait or be careful, and he was grateful for that. He wasn't a little boy anymore.

Cale took off and went to the top floor, searching for Blake. Time ticked down for him and he didn't like it. He had to get to this man and find out where they were holding Taylor. Back on the first floor, he spied another door and went to it. Once he'd passed through it, he pressed tight to the wall as he heard people and smelled the stench that accompanied demons.

Why would this man have demons at his home? Cautiously, he made his way down. It wasn't steps, but a smooth path. Beneath his feet, he could feel some grooves that indicated to him they often rolled heavy items up and down this path.

The sounds of feet thundering up toward him had him hiding. Men, women and even demons streaked up past him and out of the door. Alarms blared and were cut off when the door closed again. He understood what it meant—his brethren had arrived and were causing a distraction.

Soundproof door. He breathed out and began to move from his spot high up on the wall, only to find himself face to face with a fire breather. It slowly opened its mouth, a hiss escaping. Dropping to the ground, Cale threw four stars at it.

It joined him on the floor, dead. He kicked it to the side and was preparing to carry on when sparks burst to life along the back of his hand.

Electricity ran along his skin. Taylor. *"She's here!"* He moved out.

"You see her?"

"No, Roz, but I see the sparks she gives me." When he reached the bottom, there was more commotion and

three directions to pick from on where he should go next. He bolted straight. Torches lined this passageway and he ran fast, needing to find her.

The corridor spilled out into an old dungeon. *"There's an old dungeon beneath his house. I haven't found Blake yet either, but I'm looking for Taylor now. I know she's here."*

He didn't wait for any response, just went cell to cell. They were empty until he reached the end on one side. That one had a large body lying dead inside, and maintained the scent of Taylor, but she wasn't there. The man, or creature, wore all black and lay in the middle of the floor. Cale repositioned himself to get a better look at who it was.

"Tryvek is here."

"Where?" Tiarnán's question snapped with the force of a bullwhip.

"Dead in a cell."

"Someone killed him?"

"Yes. Not sure who, but he's dead."

"Once Hara finds out about this, it will get ugly fast. Find her and get the fuck out."

"On it."

Cale went back, double-checking the cells to make sure he hadn't missed anything. Out where it split, he went to his right and checked there. Nothing but more cells, this time they were holding demons, who set up a raucous cry when he walked in. With the few explosives he had, he set them to go off then went to the third opening.

This one was different. About fifty feet in, he reached another door. Thick. Steel.

Sparks flickered then died away and he searched for a way in. No discernible way he could find. He cursed fluently that Billy wasn't here, for that man could get into anything or anywhere.

"Billy?"

"Cale?"

"No time, man, I'm facing a thick door at least two feet with no way I can see to get in. Ideas?"

"Is there a window in it?"

"No."

"Check the hinge side. Where does it lead to?"

"Into the wall. It's in an underground place. Used to be an old dungeon. So the rock is a mix of kinds."

"Get through the rock, you'll find the electronics to it. Or go in on the other side and get a small hole so you can work the code."

"I don't have time, Billy. I need in fast. I don't care if they know I'm coming or not."

"Then don't go through the door. Can you get to something along one of the sides of that area?"

"There's another tunnel next to it, yes."

"Go in through that way. Blow your way in. It is less likely to have been reinforced than what's holding the door."

"Thanks."

"You okay?"

"They have my woman."

"Kill the bastards."

"I plan on it."

He whipped around, running back into the middle tunnel to one of the cells. That he got into easily and within seconds, he was ducking as the charge was set to explode.

As Billy had predicted, it made a hole and he burst through into a room that was something out of a torture movie. The types of devices he saw lying on tables were horrific. The person he saw laying on one sent him over the edge.

Cale roared in fury, releasing weapons at the demons who flew at him and raced down toward the table that held Taylor. He saw the woman who delivered their mail and another male near Taylor.

Then he had a wall of demons to deal with. He sliced, kicked and fought. His sign added in its own assistance. More demons poured in and explosions rocked the place, sending them to the floor.

Their bites burned like hell and the fireballs they launched at him were no picnic either. Out of stars, he went to his daggers.

"Should have just given up the pendant," a male spoke and the demons parted to let him through.

Daggers returned to their place and Cale drew a sword as he stared at the man before him. "You'll never get it, Kuruk."

The man stood over eight feet tall and had muscles that never seemed to end. "We always get what we want. Imagine, all of you here and leaving it unprotected."

Cale gave a feral grin. "Oh, damn. If only we'd thought about that. I saw your dead brother. Who killed him? I'd like to buy them a gift."

His gaze narrowed. "Tryvek was—"

"Shit of the lowest order, like you." He swung his sword as they continued to circle one another.

Kuruk yowled and attacked. Cale stepped up and met the strikes. Thrusting, parrying and delivering kicks, they battled. Each time he moved to where he could see Taylor, Cale faltered and Kuruk never failed to press his advantage.

Eventually, Tiarnán's words came back to him. About how he needed to focus and not think about her. He'd be no good to her dead. Power surged up through him and sparks lit him and the sword as he swung it again and again, driving Kuruk back.

A demon—one of the few who remained, most of them had vanished out another door to the back of the room—rose up and launched fire at him. His sign took the blunt of it, dissolving the flames.

Kuruk knew what he was doing and Cale had to concentrate. He spied a demon nearing Taylor. "No!" he cried, reaching for a dagger to send when the creature fell into a heap by the table.

Tiarnán flowed from invisibility to visibility and back again. Cale focused back on Kuruk, knowing that Taylor would be safe from any other attack.

"You need his help always, Cale. You're not strong enough to defeat me."

The explosion sent flames pouring in. Kuruk took a few seconds and stared at it. Cale swung, knocking free from his block for another attack and spinning in close where he flipped his hand grip and drove the sharp metal directly up. It penetrated Kuruk beneath the chin and didn't stop until it burst through the top of his skull.

He dropped, but Cale already had set his sights on the woman he'd come for. The fire was spreading exponentially fast. He went to lift her and saw she was chained there. Calling forth another weapon, he cut through the links holding her arms and legs then replaced the weapon all in one move.

Blood ran from her and he cupped her cheek. "Taylor." The smoke thickened and made it difficult to breathe.

"Move!" Tiarnán cried.

Scooping her up in his arms, he grabbed her batons as well. *"There is another door toward the back."*

"Get moving then. I'm almost there."

The tunnel wasn't smooth, but it was wide enough that it was easy to move through. They burst out into the rainy night and he turned in time to see the house's final collapse. The faint sounds of gunfire reached them and he also heard dogs barking. Over it all however, he identified the familiar sound of a chopper.

Together they ran to an opening and waited. Out of the clouds and rain she appeared, handling it like it was nothing. Aminta lowered and they hopped in. She never actually touched the ground, more hovered. The second Tiarnán joined them, she lifted off again and he turned his attention to the woman in his arms.

She lay there, unresponsive.

"Come on, babe." He sent what healing he could to her. Placing his head against hers, he grabbed her close to him. *Don't leave me.*

Her heartbeat was slow and sporadic. He pulled back and stared at her beneath the soft, interior helo lights. Blood mingled with her rain-soaked clothing and the anger began anew. The sparks danced along his skin, however when they moved to her they began to fade.

Not a good sign.

He lifted her shirt and growled low at the sight of her injuries. These were only the ones he could see now—he knew there were more. Tiarnán unfolded a few blankets and laid them out. Reluctantly, he placed her there.

"Arm."

He moved to Taylor's other side and grabbed her arm. *Forgive me, babe.* With a sharp move, he straightened out her broken arm, wincing at the sound of the bones grating before settling into their proper place. She remained lifeless.

Through eyes blurry with unshed tears, he gazed to Tiarnán. The unreadable mask was in place, but it was then Cale noticed a gaping wound on his side.

"You're injured."

The man hadn't said anything to him about it.

Tiarnán followed his gaze to the open injury and shrugged. "Tend her first, she's your mate."

Yes, she was and would be forever. However, they also needed all the Guardians. Tiarnán took the choice from him by moving to the front and sitting in the co-pilot's seat as Aminta flew.

Cale lay beside her, wrapping her in his arms as well as the mist of his sign. Pressing his lips to her temple, he healed her best he could. It wouldn't be enough, but it would keep her alive until they got back.

No more pussy-footing around, he was making sure she knew how much meant to him.

* * * *

She stirred and opened her eyes. Today there was more energy in her and she had the urge to get up and move about. Glancing around, she recognized her location—Cale's room. She'd spent enough nights in here to know what it looked like. What was odd, was the fact she identified some of her personal things in there.

When she'd woken, she'd always been alone, but she knew that Cale had been near. His scent surrounded her, calmed her, soothed her. She glanced down and smiled at the sight of one of his gray shirts covering her.

"Welcome back, babe."

The man she'd just been thinking about strode into view, carrying a tray that he set down at the foot of the bed. She licked her lips as she took in his appearance. His tight shirt and jeans that rode low on his lean hips did things to her that informed her she was well on her way to recovery. His dark brown hair hung forward, shielding one eye. She wanted to get up and brush it back so she could see both. Then kiss him. Run her fingers along his physique and relearn the feel of his body.

He stood alongside her and cupped her upturned face in his hands. She held her breath as he moved closer. When their lips met, she opened beneath his quest willingly. His tongue slid along hers, engaging her to tangle with him. She leaned into his touch, plastering one hand against his chest, taking comfort in the steady beat of his heart thumping beneath her palm.

Cale ended the kiss and captured her chin in one hand. "I have something to tell you."

A moment of panic set in. "Who's hurt? Did they get the pendant? Did—"

He covered her mouth with one hand. "Everyone's fine."

She dodged free, feeling much better. "Of course. X-Men win, it's what they do."

He arched an eyebrow and she made the motion of zipping her lips. He shook his head but didn't hide the smile. "I moved you into my room, which I'm sure you can tell. I am so sorry, you were taken, Taylor. I wish—"

She slapped one of her hands over his lips, halting his words. To hell with not saying anything until he'd finished. It wasn't going to happen, she wouldn't allow him to shoulder the blame for what happened. "No way, Cale. Don't blame yourself for that. It was

Haley. That had been her purpose, to get close to me so she could take me back with her."

He gently removed her hand. "Why? Why would she do that?"

"She was born into it. Her father is some being named Hara."

His expression could have been carved out of ice. "What did you say?"

"Hara. Did you catch her? She was there. Along with Blake and they were worried about a man named Lamar. Well, more Blake was. She seemed to think her father was one of the beings you wanted to kill."

"We didn't catch either of them, they must have slipped out." He nudged her over and sat on the bed beside her, gathering her close.

"That Tryvek thing was still dead though, right?"

"You met Tryvek?"

She shuddered at the memory. "I killed him. Or at least I think I did."

His lips brushed the top of her head. "He's dead all right. You did that?"

"Baton through the eye." She shrugged. "Who knew."

"When I think about how I could have lost you," he began. "No, let me talk, Taylor. It tears me apart. It's why you're here in my room. I want you to stay. Forever. In my room. At the vineyard." He cleared his throat. "With me."

She tipped her head back and peered at him. "With you?

"Only me." He traced her lips with his fingers. "I love you, Taylor. I think I've half been in love with you since the first time I saw you."

Her heart kicked up. "Because of the thing that just happened?"

"Because of who you are, Taylor Kenyon. Nothing other than that." He kissed her tenderly. "Because of what you represent, to me."

She broke their eye connection and stared across the room. "I'm no one special, Cale."

"You are to me, Taylor. To me, you're the world."

He put her on his lap and she rubbed at the skin just under the cast on her arm. She wanted to wind her arms around him, but she couldn't, so she rested her head against his chest.

"I love you, too, Cale. I want to stay here with everyone. With you."

His kiss dominated her and she arched into him, body burning for more. When he pulled back she whimpered in frustration. She wanted him, his thick cock inside her. Delivering her to the heights she knew he would.

"Cale," she begged.

He readjusted them so she lay between his legs and wrapped his arms around her. "I want you too, but you're still recovering."

Like hell. She refused to be deterred and took his hand, moving it under the blankets, to settle it over her pussy. She only wore his shirt and a pair of underwear.

"Does that feel like I need more recovery?"

She knew she was wet and ground against his hand. He groaned and rubbed her. Taylor nearly purred and widened her legs, grasping his wrist to keep him there.

"You're killing me," he swore.

Cale readjusted his hand and slipped his fingers beneath the material. She moaned aloud as he skimmed her sensitive flesh. He began to tease her, up and down her slit he moved. Brushing her clit and almost—*almost*—entering her. But he didn't. She writhed and begged, whimpered and cried, yet he refused to allow her to reach that peak.

"Tell me again," he whispered, bringing her tight to his chest, nipping the side of her throat. "Tell me the words."

"I love you."

"Once more."

"I love you, Cale Mattox."

He entered her with two thick fingers and she bucked her hips up into his hand, driving him farther inside her. The palm of his hand pressed against her clit and as he began to move, she crested. It didn't take much. Just him. His touch. His love. She rode out her orgasm and Cale didn't let her off with just one. He gave her more than that. She slumped against him, exhausted, and he kissed her again.

"I'm not letting you go, Taylor."

She smiled into the crook of his neck. "Good. I'd hate to get kidnapped again just so you could come rescue me."

She fell asleep that way and when she woke, he lay in the bed with her and she rested upon his bare chest.

"The others want to see you," he said, his hand smoothing up and down her back.

She moved the fingers of her broken arm. "Do we have to go now? I was hoping we could figure out how much more I could do with a broken arm."

His gaze turned fiery hot as he grinned. "They can wait."

About the Author

Aliyah Burke is an avid reader and is never far from pen and paper (or the computer). She is married to a career military man, and they have a German Shepherd, two Borzois, and a DSH cat. Her days are spent sharing her time between work, writing, and dog training.

Aliyah Burke loves to hear from readers. You can find her contact information, website details and author profile page at http://www.totallybound.com.

Totally Bound Publishing